Worlds
Without
Number

Books by David R. Christensen

(ages 3-5)
Tivoli's Christmas

(ages 6-8)
The Mystery of the Grinning Buddha
The Mystery of the Ugly Bottle
The Mystery of the Haunted Lighthouse

(young adult, adult fiction)
Worlds Without Number

(adult non-fiction)
Compound Words

Forthcoming

(ages 6-8)
Stanley Billings: That's Me

(adult fiction)
The Goldilocks Weight

Worlds Without Number

by
David R. Christensen

Published by
Press Forward Press
Fiction Division
5060 S 710 West
Salt Lake City, UT 84123

Text copyright © 2014 by
David R. Christensen
Cover layout and design copyright © 2014 by
Bud Spencer/SUMO Graphics

Printed in the United States of America
March 2014

Library of Congress Cataloging-in-Publication Data

Christensen, David R.
    Worlds without number/by Press Forward Press and
David R. Christensen. 1st ed.
        p.   cm.
    ISBN-13: 978-1-940802-02-2 (Paper back)
    ISBN-13: 978-1-940802-03-9 (eBook)
    1. Science fiction 2. Young adult. I. Christensen, David
R., Worlds without number. II. Press forward press. III. Title:
Worlds without number.
    813.6

Library of Congress Control Number: 2013921900

To
Michael A. Neider
&
Robert L. Pugmire

Table of Contents

Chapter One

THE YEAR 2053: SALT LAKE CITY: BLAKE

Blake froze in place at the sound of the front door slamming behind him. "Well, that discussion is over, once and for all," he whispered decisively.

He lingered on the porch just long enough to fasten his winter coat and to snuggle tightly inside. The plume of moist breath and the finality of his muttered words blended uneasily as he headed resolutely down the front steps.

"Dad pushed too far, this time. In fact, maybe I won't go on a mission at all. But regardless, I *will not* drop out of school and spend an entire year taking institute classes!"

With that settled, Blake added with disgust, "Why is today's high temperature supposed to only reach 12 degrees Fahrenheit? Is the entire world against me on Christmas morning—even the weather?"

As if on cue, the wind kicked up. Swirling gusts nudged clumps of snow off the boughs of the pine trees that lined the twisting sidewalk leading from his house to the street.

Blake managed to dodge most of them as he leaned into the blowing snow and pressed his way to the curb. He glanced up and saw the soft, inviting glow of blue light emanating from within his car.

As Blake approached his car he heard a familiar clicking sound. The door unlocked and opened upward. Blake brushed snow from his hair and coat; then he slid inside and the door closed silently beside him. His head dropped onto the soft, padded steering wheel and he exhaled deeply.

"I'm sorry," Psi said.

"I'm okay," Blake responded to the electronic device which, at the moment, he felt much closer to than to any human, such as his father.

Blake had written the life-like, human-sounding biochip-based master-App program during his senior year of high school. He had named its human personality: Psi. Blake installed it on his super smart phone and on its own remote pocket device.

Blake's work with artificial intelligence had earned him several local and state awards as well as significant national and international recognition. More important, it had earned him a five-year, all-expenses-paid scholarship to the very prestigious IPI: the International Polytechnic Institute.

Each biochip program he had ever engineered had been so logical to design that Blake hadn't realized, until they began drawing attention, that he had discovered and ingeniously utilized unique concepts related to artificial intelligence.

Blake seldom thought about all the attention he had received—especially not now. He had more important things on his mind, such as the perpetual impasse he and his father had regarding his serving a mission.

Blake mumbled to himself, "Why must Dad insist on me going on a mission, anyway? Even if I was inclined to serve, I couldn't go for another three and a half years."

"You know the answer to that," Psi responded.

"No, I don't," Blake snapped. "And why did he have to bring it up again during my winter break from school? I came home to relax and have some fun skiing. Now he spoiled all that."

"*He* spoiled it?" Psi countered.

"Yeah," Blake stated emphatically. "I thought everyone would sleep in when the family Christmas party ran so late. After all, the gifts were exchanged and opened last night. If Dad hadn't gotten up early today, I would have had breakfast at my best friend's house and headed up to Brighton Ski Resort. Instead, I'm on my way to Brighton, Michigan."

"It seems to me that that is your decision, Blake. And it would be inappropriate to blame your father for something that is the consequence of one of your own choices."

Blake didn't respond. He felt somewhat ill at ease at receiving reproof from a computer program he had designed. If he hadn't suspected he himself was in the wrong he might have tried to argue the point. Besides, no matter how much Blake might want to think Psi was an independent voice, he knew Psi was actually a voice from within his own mind, a second conscience.

"Okay, Psi. I don't feel like arguing with you."

"Now that could be a fun experiment. Just think, to debate with me is to battle with yourself and in the end you would have to deal with being a winner and a loser," Psi stated with a human-like, though computer-generated, chuckle.

Blake lifted his head. He rubbed the shallow indentation made by the steering wheel. "I'm ready to go, Psi. Would you drive?"

"Certainly, Blake."

The windshield wipers strained momentarily beneath the several inches of snow that had accumulated since Blake arrived home from school the day before.

When the last of the snow had been cleared away, the automobile's motor began to hum. Psi skillfully shifted power between the four wheels. The car gradually moved forward into the rutted snow that blanketed the street.

"Where are we headed?" Psi asked. "Is it Brighton, Utah or Brighton, Michigan?"

Blake rehearsed in his mind the frustrated feelings resulting from the conversation he had just had with his father. The excitement of skiing had vanished. At the moment, he simply wanted to get as far away from home as possible.

"On to Michigan. But first let's stop at the nearest Power-Up Mart."

"I do not detect a need to recharge our batteries," Psi declared.

Blake exhaled slowly, his patience already worn thin. "This visit to the Power-Up Mart is not about you, nor is it about the vehicle over which you currently have charge. It's about me and right now I need a chocolate-covered Pershing and some chocolate milk. I did miss breakfast, you know."

"I am aware of that, Blake. I also know you are capable of making better breakfast choices."

Blake sighed deeply. "Sometimes I think my mother must have found a way to reprogram you—to be more like her."

"I'll take that as a compliment," Psi replied, not intimidated in the least.

"You would," Blake said dryly. Then shaking his head he added, "I suppose it is a compliment, at that."

"Actually, since she is the only mother you will ever have, simply consider me to be a very humble, all-wise assistant, advisor, counselor, and mentor."

Blake shuddered. "Do you really see yourself that way?"

"Perhaps not entirely, but with instant access to an almost unlimited amount of information, coupled with a flawless comprehension and assimilation of that knowledge through my processors, I am an outstanding match for anything you might choose to discuss or debate."

"Yeah, right," Blake stated skeptically.

"Here we are," Psi announced as he eased the car to a stop in front of one of several covered Power-Up pumps that encircled the round, glass-enclosed kiosk. "I figured since we are here, I might as well bring the car's batteries up to a full charge."

"Whatever sparks your transistors," Blake said as he hopped out of the car and began pushing his way through the wind-blown snow.

"Transistors, indeed," Psi remarked repulsively. "How archaic!"

Blake shook the snow from his coat before entering the store. For the briefest moment he considered what Psi had suggested regarding breakfast food, then headed straight for the pastry closet. He removed two chocolate-covered Pershings, wrapped them in several tissues, and placed them into a paper sack. He pulled two chugs of chocolate milk from the dairy chest and made his way to the front counter.

He placed his purchases on the scanner and slipped his credit/ID card into a slot.

After pressing two selection buttons, a delightful female voice listed his purchases including the cost to bring his car up to full charge. The total appeared on a read-out screen. Blake pressed his left thumb on a flashing square and a soft bell chimed.

"Thank you Blake," the voice said sweetly. Then the voice buttons went blank, ready for the next customer to choose a preferred age and gender for the electronic clerk.

Despite Blake's passion for designing life-like computer programs, he had never become accustomed to electronic clerks. "You're welcome," he half-mumbled as he shook his head. He placed the sack of pastry and bottles of milk into a plastic bag. "I can't believe I still talk with sales computers."

The voice buttons blinked back on. "I sympathize with you, Blake," the feminine voice replied, "but have you ever considered just how good you make us feel when you do?"

Blake refused to respond. Once outside the Power-Up Mart, he plowed his way through the pelting snow, making a beeline for the car.

As he reached for the handle, the door opened and Blake hastily removed his coat, stuffed it behind the driver's seat, and slipped inside.

Psi said, "I'm a computer and you still talk to me."

"What?!" Blake exclaimed. "You couldn't have heard

what I said to that electronic clerk. I was still in the kiosk."

Psi directed the backing of the car and maneuvered it onto the sparsely occupied street. "You underestimate the sensitivity of my auditory receivers. Your roommate made very significant improvements on them just before winter break. You were in the shower at the time."

Blake smiled to himself. "That sounds just like Roger. I wonder why he never mentioned it."

"He told me it was a surprise Christmas gift. He asked me not to say anything about it until it was appropriate to do so."

"Merry Christmas to you too, Roger," Blake mused as he grabbed the bag from the passenger's seat.

"I know you failed to take my advice, Blake. That sack contains virtually no nutritious food."

"How can you be so sure?" Blake asked as he peered into the bag he pulled to his face.

"It contains precisely two chocolate-glazed Pershings and two one-pint chugs of whole chocolate milk. I process all your purchases. You should know that."

Blake shook his head. "Oh, I do. I just keep hoping you will forget once in a while," he said, pressing a button. The steering wheel folded onto the steering column and both slipped into the dashboard. A food-serving tray emerged from a slot in the car door and rotated until it was horizontal.

He withdrew a Pershing and a bottle of chocolate milk from the plastic bag, placed the sack with the remaining Pershing on the seat next to him, and stowed the second chug of chocolate milk in the small refrigerator in front of the passenger's seat. "Why don't you simply concentrate on driving?"

"See. I was right," Psi said.

"Of course you were," Blake responded nonchalantly. After taking a bite of Pershing and washing it down with chocolate milk, he continued. "Now, just how far can you hear?"

"That information is classified. But this much I will tell you. I can easily hear from a recharging pump to the inside of a Power-Up Mart."

Psi directed the car from 1300 East onto Interstate 80, eastbound. Immediately, the ride became smoother and quieter. Road-heating systems had recently been installed in all interstate highways. Moderately-heavy snowfall quickly evaporated. Heavy snowfall resulted in nothing more than damp pavement.

A few minutes later, Blake turned to his left and looked out the window. He hoped to see deer foraging along the lower slopes of the mountains that flanked Parleys Canyon.

The next several minutes passed in silence. Then Psi said, "We're approaching Kimball Junction. Would you consider skiing Deer Valley, perhaps? Or if you've changed your mind about leaving home in such a huff, this would be a good place to turn around."

"I haven't changed my mind, Psi," Blake declared,

and then added with a grumble, "In a huff, was it?"

"You have been so quiet, I thought perhaps you were reconsidering your destination."

"Wrong, Psi. See, you are not infallible."

"I never said I was, nor do I think I am," Psi said defensively. When Blake did not respond, Psi softly added, "Darn near, though."

Blake laughed. "I was just waiting to see how long you could handle me not reacting to your last comment." Blake laughed again.

Psi changed the subject. "So, why were you so quiet if it had nothing to do with turning back?"

"I was wondering how far Roger had extended your hearing. Classified, you said? By whom? Roger can't control whether or not you tell me how far you can hear."

"Says who?"

"Says me. You are first and foremost my computer program and I have installed plenty of safeguards to prevent anyone from tampering with you."

"Roger *is* pretty smart, you know," Psi said.

"Obviously," Blake said as he shrugged. "So, how did he do it? The Psi *I* programmed could not have picked up sound that far away, especially during a snowstorm."

"And yet I did hear," Psi said. "Is there some reason why you are so concerned with how far I can detect sounds?"

"Can you hear as far as from the curb in front of my house to the living room?" Blake asked sternly.

Psi paused awhile. "Under normal conditions, I believe I could."

"*Normal conditions*? You *believe you could*?" Blake replied incredulously.

"Today there were abnormal conditions, Blake. You know—the blizzard—the howling wind—the snow smothering the car? That was not normal."

Blake exhaled heartily. "That's a relief."

"What's a relief?" Psi asked.

"I was thinking I might be embarrassed if you had heard what was said during my—a—tiff with my dad."

"Oh, I would hardly call it a tiff," Psi said. "No, it was more like an argument, an altercation, a blowup, a knock-down-and-drag-out, a...."

Blake cut Psi off. "Hold it! You said you couldn't hear things from within my living room during a blizzard."

"Actually, I said I thought I could *under normal conditions*," Psi stated.

"This morning's conditions were hardly normal. You said so yourself. So, how could you know if it was a tiff, a squabble, or an out-and-out dispute?"

"Don't forget, Blake, you and your dad have been arguing for a long time about you serving a mission."

"So you've overheard bits and pieces here and there for months."

"A little over a year, actually."

"That still doesn't explain how you knew the conversation I had with my dad this morning ended up heated, does it?"

"No," Psi said. "But the fact that the wind obstructed my hearing does not mean I know nothing of what was said, and yelled, inside your house."

Blake inhaled deeply in preparation for his counter-remark, but Psi spoke first.

"Look Blake, the fact is I know everything that was said and done this morning—in the living room of your house."

"How could you?" Blake demanded.

"I know because I witnessed it all."

Chapter Two

NEXT STOP: CHEYENNE

"Coalville is coming up," Psi said.

"Don't change the subject," Blake insisted.

"I didn't mean to change the subject. I was simply stating a fact that could be important and if not considered now might be too late in a minute or so."

Blake rubbed his chin. "Okay. But I still think you were changing the subject."

"Not really," Psi began, "but shall I take us on past Coalville?"

"Yes, Psi. Perhaps I'll change my mind later about going all the way to Michigan. But for now, I am more interested in how you knew what was going on in my

13

house this morning. Can you see and hear what is happening in anybody's house? That thought is scary."

"Blake, you programmed me to be discriminating and prudent. I know only what went on in *your* living room this morning because I knew you were facing a difficult situation with your father. I chose to listen in."

Blake twisted the kink out of his neck. "Oh, all right," he said impatiently. "But, how did you do it?"

Psi didn't respond.

Blake's voice softened. "Come on, Psi. It's okay. I admit I trust you to make appropriate decisions. I promise I won't be upset," Blake added reassuringly.

"Okay, Blake. You know I have wireless capabilities, don't you?"

"Of course. All computers do."

"Did you know that the typical person never turns his computer off?"

"Yeah, that's standard procedure. But what does that have to do with anything?"

"Think, Blake. Whenever the power to any of your family's computers is left on, I can connect with them wirelessly. This morning I tapped into the computer monitor in your living room and turned on the webcam. I witnessed everything."

"But how were you so certain something would happen between my dad and me this morning? I know I switched off your remote App," Blake said as he removed it from his shirt pocket and pressed the button at the bottom. "See, the App is still in sleep mode."

14

"I bypassed the sleep-mode setting. It's not all that difficult. I simply connected directly to your living room computer."

"What!" Blake snapped. "Have you done this before?"

"No, no. I have had no occasion to, nor any interest in doing so, until this morning. Even then the main reason I tuned in was because I sensed a confrontation between you and your dad."

Blake was bewildered. "Really?"

"Yes. Now, as far as me listening inappropriately, you programmed propriety into me, remember?"

"Of course I do. So, how did you *sense* me and my dad heading for, let's say, a heated discussion?"

"I noted an increase in your heart rate, blood pressure, brain wave agitation—things like that."

"Yuck, Psi. You're creeping me out. And this is why you chose to spy on me today?" Blake said cringing.

"*Spy* is such a harsh word," Psi responded.

"I'm sorry my word choice doesn't meet with your approval. I'm having a difficult time adjusting to this new, expanded role of yours...," Blake said, "...this enhanced interest you have in me and my dad."

"The New Testament counsels everyone to love his neighbor. In that sense, you are my neighbor. Hey, you know what, Blake? I might very well be your first missionary convert but, although I am waterproof, I doubt that I am baptizable."

Psi waited. Blake did not laugh. He didn't even crack

a smile, but coldly responded, "My first and only convert."

"I was trying to be funny—to help you relax. Anyway, I have stored in my memory everything about religion. So I know it is not good that you and your dad are at odds about, let's say, your educational and spiritual future."

"You're on my dad's side!" Blake cried out. "You too think I should serve a mission before completing my schooling. Didn't I program you to be my friend?"

"Blake, I am your friend and always will be."

Blake plowed his fingers through his hair, wondering if grabbing a couple of handfuls and yanking hard could possibly make him feel any worse. "It is shocking enough to learn you listened in, in the first place—but taking sides? How could you?"

"Actually, Blake, it might help if after you calm down you were to review your interaction with your dad."

"What possible good could that do, Psi?"

"You might learn something that softens your heart or modifies your point of view."

Blake frowned. "I doubt it, Psi."

"My purpose wasn't to be nosey, let alone to take sides. I thought that, just maybe, if you watched this morning's experience from a step or two away, you might learn something beneficial."

"Wait a second," Blake stated forcefully. "You just said I could *watch* me and my dad. When you said a few minutes ago that you witnessed it all, I thought maybe you could play back the audio."

"I could do that," Psi said matter-of-factly. "But since I listened in by means of the webcam, I also have the video. I could even project it holographically, if you'd like."

"You could do that?"

"Certainly."

"How did you obtain that technical capability?" Blake inquired.

"One day I realized it could be done, so I figured out how to do it and programmed it into myself," Psi explained.

In frustration, Blake grabbed the sack containing the second Pershing and snatched the other chug of chocolate milk from the refrigerator.

"Tsk, tsk," Psi clicked pathetically.

"Hey, Psi, it tastes good. Besides, *you,* who know me oh-so-well, must know that I eat when I am nervous or upset."

"Would you be interested in knowing that you have put on two tenths of a pound since you got up this morning?"

"No, Psi. I am not interested in my weight changes— up or down. But thanks to you I am feeling even more upset now and more likely to keep eating junk food."

"I just wanted to help, Blake," Psi replied meekly.

"Oh, I know, Psi, but at the moment I feel a little beyond that sort of help. That's why I'm eating junk food. Okay?"

"Okay. But I still want to know if you would let me replay this morning's encounter with your dad? In the long run it might help relieve some of your anxiety."

"I'm not struggling with anxiety," Blake retorted. "Whatever gave you that idea?"

"I'm glad you asked. First: your behavior. And second: your vital signs. I check them periodically and when they reach certain levels, I monitor them continually."

"Where are we, Psi?" Blake asked in an attempt to end that topic.

"We have just entered Wyoming. Thanks to the new I-80 design for speeds of 180 mph, we will be in Cheyenne in an hour and fifty-seven minutes."

"The stress of dealing with this morning is making me sleepy, Psi. Would you wake me up just before we are to reach Cheyenne?"

"Certainly, Blake. Would you like to listen to some soft music until you fall asleep?"

"That would be great. I'll leave it up to you to select what you think is best."

In about two minutes, Blake had fallen into deep sleep to Chopin's *Nocturne in E flat Major*, which had melodiously filled the car.

"Blake. We're approaching Cheyenne," Psi said quietly.

Blake awoke to the very note of Chopin that had played just before he was overtaken with sleep.

Blake didn't understand how this *biochip-child* of his

18

had acquired the ability to know the exact moment his programmer fell asleep, but Blake appreciated hearing the complete nocturne, even though it was split into two parts by his slumber.

"Pull off at the next Power-Up Mart. I feel a little stiff and I'd like to stretch my legs."

"Shall I recharge the batteries and replenish the fuel-cell supply tanks?" Psi asked.

"We shouldn't be low yet," Blake said as the car approached a Power-Up pump.

"We aren't. But on our last trip back to school, you chose to drive straight through from Cheyenne to Des Moines."

"That's right, Psi," Blake acknowledged. "Well, since we've stopped I see no sense in stopping again. Sure, go ahead."

Blake climbed out of the car and into the blowing snow. He hadn't been aware of the weather for the past two hours, but he assumed it had snowed all of the way to Cheyenne. If the wind had raged, as it often did, he missed that as well and that was okay.

Blake ran for the door of the quick-service store. Inside, a single light moved above the head of the attendant who looked up, stopped stocking shelves, and repositioned himself behind the counter, where the light above him stopped as well.

The moment Blake entered the store, all the lights came on.

"So when are they going to automate this kiosk?"

Blake asked. "I stop here every time I pass through Cheyenne and I ask the same question each time to whoever happens to be behind the counter. You're new."

A young man about Blake's age, who was seated behind the counter, said, "The owners say they can't justify the expense. It's not like we do as much business as the ones in the big cities."

"And that's the same answer I get each time," Blake said. "Frankly, when I stop to buy something, I prefer speaking with a real person anyway."

"Thank you—say you're one of those students from IPI, aren't you?" the store clerk said.

Blake nodded toward his car, which was parked next to a Power-Up pump. "They're a dead giveaway, aren't they?"

"And you're halfway through your sophomore year."

Blake stopped perusing the candy counter and faced the attendant. "You must have had a lot of students stop here."

"Not really. But I know my cars. Yours is second-year issue."

The readout on the customer screen flicked from red to green. The attendant glanced at the monitor and seemed surprised. "Where are you coming from today, may I ask?"

"Salt Lake City. I left there this morning—about two and a half hours ago."

The attendant looked shocked. "This isn't your first stop for a recharge, is it?"

Blake nodded.

"I don't get it. That's too far for a single charge."

Blake explained. "The body design of cars for lower-class students is boring and we're not permitted to change it. But we are allowed to modify whatever we want, however we want, on the inside."

"And your car can go 440 miles on a single charge?"

"Actually, it can go about 700 miles," Blake said casually.

"And you made this change yourself?"

"No. My roommate did. Roger is a quite the genius at mechanical theory and application. My specialty is computers and programming them to function as much as possible like humans."

"I wish I was good at things like that," the boy said, a little envy in his voice. "But, the only real decent grades I ever got in high school were in auto-shop."

Blake said, "The world will always need mechanics."

"Oh, with all the new computer gadgets under the hood, I can't understand much of any of that. I specialized in auto body design and repair."

"I bet that that was interesting, what with fiberglass, carbon fiber, all the new alloys...."

"I don't work with any of those."

"Okay, I'll stop guessing. What do you do with car bodies?" Blake asked.

"My great-grandpa Glen began collecting antique cars when he was my age. Eventually, he had two buildings behind his house full of dozens of old, restored antique cars. You know, Model A's and Model T's—cars from the early twentieth century. He even had a 1958 Ford Edsel and a 1962 Studebaker Avanti. These two buildings were like personal museums."

"So, you work along side of him?"

"No, he died not long before I was born. But I was named Glen—after him."

"I'm glad to meet you. My name is Blake."

"My grandfather inherited all his dad's cars. Now, he's teaching me how to restore relics of the past—from the chassis up and the interior out. As far as the bodywork goes, we work almost exclusively with sheet metal."

"Fascinating."

"Right now, my grandpa and I are working on a very rare automobile. About ninety years ago, his father got a hold of one of only five known 1929 Hudson Phaetons. It was the only one known to be in the United States. He restored it. It is a beautiful car."

"I'd love to see it some day."

"It gets better. A few years ago, my grandpa learned that an elderly lady, right here in Cheyenne, had a 1929 Phaeton just sitting in her garage. It had been sitting on blocks since her father died sixty years ago.

"Grandpa bought it from her. You might think it was in perfect condition, you know, the unscratched, low-mileage, immaculate car belonging to a little old lady. You would be wrong. Her father almost drove it into the ground. He was a traveling salesman. It was so beat up that she just left it there in the garage."

"And your grandfather and you are restoring it?"

"Exactly. It's taking a long time, but that's okay. Restoring old cars seems to be what I was cut out to do," Glen said.

"I'd love to see both Hudsons. In fact, I'd love to tour both museums," Blake said as he turned around to do his shopping.

A few minutes later, Blake returned to the front counter. Glen began sliding each item across the scanner.

Immediately, Blake's super smart phone buzzed and vibrated vehemently.

Without waiting for Blake to respond, Psi announced disgustedly, "Really, Blake. Let me see, two more Pershings, four candy bars, a package of Twinkies, a large bag of Sunchips...."

"Stop, Psi! I'm hungry, okay?"

"There is a fruit closet..."

"Now, after this uncalled for interruption, I'm feeling even more frustrated."

"...behind the cookie shelf. Did you see it?"

"No! I wasn't looking for it, nor did I notice the cookie shelf."

"Would you like me to list totals for calories, cholesterol, sodium, and...?"

"No, Psi. I would not!"

"May I calculate how much weight this purchase will

put on your body, how soon you will incur a stomach ache, and how long the pain will last?"

"Absolutely not! When I get back to school I'll start eating better, okay? Oh, I need one more item—some Oreos. Thanks for the cookie-shelf reminder, Psi."

The attendant's jaw had dropped open and his head slowly shook. "Is someone slumped down in your car and talking with you on the phone?"

"It's my biochip buddy. He speaks through a special App I designed for my science fair project during my last year of high school. My roommate and I have the only two. It's what secured my scholarship to IPI."

The attendant placed Blake's purchases into a plastic bag and Blake handed him his scholarship voucher card.

As Blake started to leave, he glanced at the business card Glen had just given him.

"Thanks. If I'm not in a huge hurry, I'll stop by the next time I'm on my way to or from Salt Lake City."

"I look forward to it," Glen replied.

Blake slipped out into the blustering snow and hurried to his car.

Chapter Three

ON TO DES MOINES

When the door was fully open, he tossed his new bag of goodies onto the passenger seat, brushed the snow off his shirt, and seated himself behind the steering wheel.

The car scrunched through the snow, pulled cautiously out into traffic, and headed for the nearest eastbound I-80 on-ramp.

With the food tray positioned in front of him, Blake filled it with his culinary treasures. "Oh, rats. I forgot to get something to drink," Blake said complaining.

Psi responded. "And?"

"Darn it, Psi. Why didn't you remind me? Oh, I remember now. You were too busy criticizing my food choices," Blake said. "You probably assumed my beverage selection would be equally lousy."

Blake considered the food on the tray. "It really looks yummy, Psi, but you were right—crummy choices. And my stomach is beginning to hurt from the stuff I ate a few hours ago. When will I ever learn?"

Psi didn't respond verbally, but pulled into the parking lot of the local 24/365 Supermarket.

Blake put his precious food back into the sack, reached behind the seat, and grabbed his coat. The car door opened and Blake bailed out, running for the front door.

Several minutes later he returned. As the car reentered the roadway, Blake opened the shopping bag and pulled out the results of his most recent shopping adventure.

"You went to the deli. Hmm. Turkey breast on rye with lettuce, tomato, and alfalfa sprouts—a very good choice. And an apple and an orange and a bottle of spring water. Well, scramble my biochips," Psi said in conclusion.

The car approached the acceleration lane and soon merged with the sparse freeway traffic. A few minutes later Blake was traveling at top speed, and with comfort-control turned on Blake began lunch with a ride as smooth and steady as if at his mother's dining room table.

Psi did not disturb Blake as he ate. But when Blake was finished, he said, "How do you feel now that you've eaten sensibly for the first time today?"

"Psi, I know you're right. It's just that sometimes I eat because I'm feeling down. My stomach does feel better though. Thank you for pulling off the road long enough for me to run into that grocery store. Are you going to be upset if I snack a little bit once in awhile on the—a—junk food I bought at the Power-Up Mart?"

"Blake, I wouldn't have been upset if you had refused to enter that supermarket and told me to get on with my prime objective—getting you away from Salt Lake City."

Blake wiped his lips with a napkin. "Yum, that was delicious."

"We have a three and a half hour drive to Des Moines," Psi said. "Is there any particular way you would like to pass the time?"

"I think I know what you would suggest—watching the video of my dad and me *discussing* things this morning. It might prove amusing at that."

"Perhaps you have forgotten what took place, Blake. I don't think you will find it funny at all. I didn't. But the nice thing is that anytime you want me to discontinue showing it, all you have to do is say *stop, pause,* or *save.*"

"Or *delete*," Blake said with a slight chuckle. "Okay, let's give it a try."

"I'll begin it with the first words your father said when he came downstairs this morning. Is that all right?"

27

"Suits me," Blake said.

Good morning, Blake. Did you sleep well last night?
Did you, Dad?
I have slept better.

"Observe how you answered your dad's question with a question. Can't you tell he has something on his mind?" Psi asked.

"Sure I can, and I did then. I just didn't want to get into what about me and my life worries him and affects his life so terribly."

"Even though his worries are you?"

"Especially since his worries are me. But I and a mission are my concerns. They shouldn't be his."

"It's not that cut and dry, Blake," Psi said.

Blake, I would like to continue discussing you and your mission.

What? My mission?! I haven't even decided to go on a mission. In fact, each time you bring it up I feel less like going on one of those things. Please stop bugging me about it, okay?

Look, Blake, it's just that I phoned IPI a week ago....

What! Why, Dad?!

I wanted to know their policy on a student withdrawing temporarily for reasons such as serving a mission.

Oh, Dad. Can't you just stay out of it?

Blake, have you ever checked into their policy.

No, Dad. I haven't. Why would I? Can't you understand that I want to complete all five years of college before I tackle anything else? Getting that scholarship was the best thing that ever happened to me. Thousands of kids would give an arm or a leg to have the opportunity I have been given. I don't want to lose it.

I realize that, and I believe I understand your position, Blake—I really do. But...."

But what, Dad?

I wish I had followed your schedule more closely during the past year and a half. I just happened to see an email printout from IPI on your mother's dresser the other day.

And...?

You aren't enrolled in Spanish.

Is that all you noticed? How about me getting straight A's? How about those A+s? Please, Dad, can't you leave things alone? I'm doing just fine.

"Notice how your dad was slow to respond to each of your last few comments. He knows the conversation isn't going well and he's afraid you are about to explode—again. So was I, for that matter."

29

"But, I didn't, Psi, not this time anyway. But he kept pushing me, honest."

"Let's watch and see."

Blake looked back at the screen.

Dad, where did you go on your mission, huh?
That has nothing to do with it, Blake.
Oh, yes it does. Where did you go, Dad?
You know very well.
Yes, I do know—the Mexico Villanueva Central Mission. And what language do they speak there? They speak Spanish, of course. And where did you meet Mom?

There was a pause. Blake looked up at the video screen. It hadn't stopped working.

In Villanueva, Dad. She served a fulltime mission there too. So what second language does she speak? Spanish, Dad.
The church is growing very rapidly in Mexico, Blake.
And where did Jonathan and William serve? Oh, I'll save you the trouble of answering— Peru and Chile. My parents and older brothers served in Central and South America and they all speak Spanish.
Well, they speak Portuguese in Brazil.
Oh, is that supposed to relieve the tension,

Dad?

"Your father is trying so hard, Blake. Can't you see that?"

"Sure. But he comes on so strongly, Psi. He always assumes I'm going on a mission. I can't even begin to count the number of times he has told me in one breath that I need to learn Spanish and in the next breath that Church leaders determine the places missionaries go, all under the inspiration of the Spirit, of course? Doesn't he see this is confusing?"

"I think he just wants you to have the same experiences he had of baptizing lots of people. Besides, your testimony might develop faster if you are working with those who readily accept the Gospel."

> *Blake. I wasn't trying to relieve the tension, but the Church is growing fast in all the Spanish-speaking countries of Central and South America. The chances of being called to one of those countries, is pretty good.*
>
> *It's growing fast in one Portuguese-speaking country too.*

"See your father's frustrated face as he pauses to regroup."

> *I didn't know until a few days ago that you had chosen to study Chinese. What brought*

about that change? When did that begin?

The very day I entered International Polytechnic, Dad. Did you know that the largest and most progressive and innovative car manufacturer in the world is in China? I bet you didn't know that.

No, I didn't. But let me tell you what I learned from the Dean's Office at IPI. They told me that you may drop out for a few years as long as you do it between your second and third years of school.

Dad, don't you understand that based on how I feel right now, I don't even want to go on a mission.

But you might change your mind. If you did, you could take some religion classes at the U of U Institute.

Stop, Dad. You just don't seem to be getting it. If I ever change my mind, let me do it after I graduate—in three and a half years.

By then you may not even want to go.

I don't want to go already. Bishop Walters didn't serve a mission and he's a great man. You know he and his wife are converts. They were married, with a couple kids, when they met the missionaries. And they turned out just fine.

Oh, Blake.

Okay, Dad, let's look at this from a different perspective. You're an accountant, so this should be easy for you to understand.

Okay.

Remember when you went on your mission? You were eighteen. You returned from Mexico when you were twenty. You then spent four years in college and graduated when you were twenty-four. Am I right so far?

Of course, Blake.

I finished high school when I was fifteen. If I complete my five-year vehicle-design program without interruption, I will be done when I am twenty. Boys still go on their missions when they are eighteen. If they choose to go to college for four years, they graduate at the same age you did—twenty-four.

Suppose for some strange, unforeseen reason I decide to go on a mission—after I graduate. I'd go when I am twenty, but I will already have my degree, so I will be ready to go out into the world and earn a living when I am twenty-two. Need I point out that that puts me two years ahead of you, Dad?

"At that, your father gave up and left the room."

So, Dad, is there anything wrong with that?!

"You're yelling, Blake. What is that now, about a child honoring his father that his days may be long upon

33

the land? That's Exodus 12:20 if I remember correctly."

"I'm sure you're right, Psi."

"Actually, it's Exodus 20:12. You were taught that in high school seminary when you studied the Old Testament."

"Whatever," Blake uttered dryly.

"And that was your conversation with your dad. As you stormed out of the house, he slumped down in his leather recliner."

Blake sat silently.

Finally, Psi spoke, "I'm waiting."

Blake responded sarcastically, "And I'm processing."

Psi giggled. "Did you know I could alter the dialogue and picture and play a holographic version of the discussion you and your dad had? I can even change what each of you said and how each of you reacted. I could create what might be considered the perfect interaction between a loving father and his respectful son. It might prove quite interesting and revealing to see how you two might have spoken to each other differently and with more sensitivity."

Blake squeezed his eyes closed.

"Whoops," Psi said. "I think I've said too much."

Blake faced out the window of the car. Everything whizzed by so quickly. He tried jerking his head from toward the front of the car to the back, hoping to freeze a scene from outside. It didn't work—not at 180 mph.

In his solitude, he finally did what he usually did when he was stressed. He reached for the bag of goodies he had purchased at the first stop in Cheyenne. He withdrew his favorite two candy bars: a Snickers Peanut Butter Square double pack and a Butterfinger.

Both candy bars were variations of chocolate and peanut butter. He chose the Butterfinger first. Without realizing it, he selected it so he could get the thing about toffee sticking to his teeth over and done.

He took a bite and despite having been taught to not speak with food in his mouth, he said, "So, Psi, what are your conclusions regarding the conversation between my dad and me?"

"Well, you both try way too hard to be understood, to be right, and to win. Did either of you even once acknowledge the other's position? Nope." The last word Psi spoke ended his little speech flippantly.

Blake said nothing at first as he poked at his teeth with a round toothpick. When he was finished he stated, "We really blew it, didn't we?"

Psi said, "We?"

"I suppose I should provide an accountable version, shouldn't I?"

"I would surely think so. After all, you can't change your dad, and even if you could, it wouldn't be right to do so, would it?"

"I really blew it, didn't I?"

"Yes, I believe you did," Psi said agreeing.

"But what I blew was in how I handled things. I still can't see going on a mission. I can't!"

Chapter Four

Roger paused outside the door leading into the apartment building. He gazed up at the seemingly endless façade of windows. Somewhere, up on the fifth floor, was one window of particular interest. It belonged to his old bedroom, the only bedroom he had ever had before going off to college.

He tried to recall any worthwhile memories he had had in that room. He couldn't. He scanned every memory he could think of in the entire apartment. There were no good memories in any of its rooms.

Then Roger considered the entire rundown tenement house. No happy memories. Surely he must have had some fun times with his childhood friends—none that he could remember. His thoughts reached out to the schools he had attended, to all of Brooklyn, to all of New York City. He could recall no memories worth holding on to.

Oh, there was one happy *moment* in that shamble of an apartment his parents rented, Roger was willing to concede, but just one.

It was the day he came home from school and discovered an envelope addressed to him. It was from IPI, the foremost school for the development and advancement of automotive vehicle design and function.

"Yes," Roger admitted to himself. "I was genuinely happy that afternoon."

He chuckled audibly, then he thought. *I wonder. Was I genuinely happy because I had been accepted to the college I had dreamed of attending since first becoming fascinated with cars? Yes, that did make me happy, but to be completely honest, it was because finally I had a way out of this miserable, deplorable apartment building and away from my wretched, disgusting life.*

Roger tipped his head to one side. He spoke out loud but softly—to himself. "So why in the world am I back? Hasn't everything been better since I left?"

Off down some dark and dirty alley someone screamed.

Roger's body tensed and momentarily froze in place. Then he tucked his attaché case under the arm holding a small suitcase and reached for the doorknob. Then he hurried inside.

There was nothing he could do to help the person who was screaming. He had learned *that* while still a child. Everyone in this area of Brooklyn stayed busy—minding their own business. Besides, how could he call for help? He had left his super smart phone and the remote pocket device in his car.

There was only one chance of assistance for this screaming soul. At least half a dozen people with windows facing the alley might glance out. On a good day, one of them would call the police.

They would not identify themselves, convinced that their civic duty extended no further than the phone call.

Roger glanced at the bank of mailboxes. He noticed the corner of a letter sticking out of the side of the box belonging to his parents.

Roger gazed up at the seemingly endless steps that led up four flights of stairs.

Oh, Roger realized, *there was a good thing that happened to me while I lived here. I wouldn't say it was a happy thing, but the workout I received each time I climbed these stairs kept my legs, lungs, and heart in pretty good condition.*

Roger paused to catch his breath on the half-landing just above the third floor. He peered out the window through a group of several missing panes of glass, the opening's edge spiked with thin broken mullions.

He leaned toward the opening, hesitant to stick his head out too far. His body jerked back as he heard two gunshots fired in rapid succession.

Now, if I were in Poughkeepsie, I could safely assume that that was a car backfiring, Roger thought. *But in this neighborhood, it was gunfire.*

Again, someone somewhere was in grave trouble. Roger redirected his thoughts, certain that once again there was nothing he could do to help. He plodded on up the stairs choosing not to stop until he had reached the fifth floor. He had opted for being out of breath over being exposed to any more neighborhood tragedies.

He paused in front of the apartment door with even more hesitation than he had felt on the stoop below. The smell of tobacco and alcohol penetrated his parents' door.

Inhaling briefly and bravely, Roger pushed the doorbell button. He didn't hear it ring inside, but fearing to aggravate his father by ringing too soon again, he waited a moment. Then Roger leaned his ear near the door and pressed the button again.

It hadn't rung. He knocked and waited. He knocked again, a little louder this time. Still there was no answer.

Roger fished his key ring out of a front pocket, selected the one with *Schlage* imprinted on it, inserted it into the lock, and urged the door open.

Instantly Roger backed away. What he had smelled in the hall was much worse inside. For a moment he considered leaving—heading back to school right then.

He had told his parents he would be arriving Christmas Day, but it seemed they had forgotten. Maybe they had remembered but simply didn't care. There was no Christmas tree—not even a small one. In fact, there was no indication of any kind suggesting that it was Christmas.

There wasn't even a note explaining when they might return from whatever *incredibly important* place they had gone.

Roger decided to take another chance at upsetting his father. Though his dad would undoubtedly fly into a rage if, when he came home, the apartment was cold, Roger opened all the windows. If he was lucky there would be enough time to air out the apartment, close the windows, and reheat the rooms before his father's return.

Roger heard a gentle rustling sound somewhere in the back of the apartment. As he walked past the sofa table, a scrawny cat appeared in the kitchen doorway. Each of its ribs stood out enough to make counting them easy.

"Is that you, Tiger?" Roger asked the shy, skinny body, covered with matted hair.

The cat stepped cautiously forward. Roger stooped down, hesitating at first even to touch the creature that reeked of urine and fecal matter.

Roger closed his eyes and tried to comprehend how his parents' household could exist in such a state of filth. He approached the kitchen sink, rolled up his sleeves, and for just a moment stared at the mess, trying to decide where to begin.

Then he simply began. He removed five empty bottles from the sink. Two were labeled whiskey, two were labeled gin, and one bore the label of a cheap wine. He placed them on the counter next to what seemed to be a week's collection of unwashed plates, coffee cups, and flatware.

Roger opened the doors below the sink, expecting to find a trash can. Had he taken a moment to think, he would have realized that even if there was one, it would probably be full of more empty liquor bottles. It was. And there were several empty beer cans in it as well.

Roger removed the trash can, walked through the apartment and out into the hall, and emptied it into the trash chute. Back at the sink Roger opened three cabinet drawers before he found a spatula he could use as a small shovel.

After a trip to the living room, Roger returned with a month-old newspaper. He slid a few dirty dishes to one side, put down the paper, and began scooping up at least two weeks' worth of discarded coffee grounds. Lastly, during another trip to the living room, he collected a half dozen overloaded ashtrays and dumped their contents on top of the coffee grounds.

Tiger mewed at Roger's feet. Roger stopped what he was doing and went to the refrigerator. He was surprised to discover a bottle containing a little fresh milk. He rinsed out a bowl, placed it on the floor, and poured in what milk was left.

With the coffee grounds and cigarette butts wrapped in paper and more empty bottles in the trash can, Roger took a second trip to the trash chute. When he returned,

41

Tiger had finished the milk and was staring up as if, having just discovered the meaning of food, surely there was more to be had. Roger shook his head. He was fairly sure there wasn't.

He looked through the cupboards hoping to find some cat food, but to no avail. He did find a can of tuna fish, however, which he decided to share with Tiger—if he could find some salad dressing and bread for himself. He checked the refrigerator and found neither, nor was there any lettuce or tomatoes.

"I guess you get the entire can, Tiger, but not all at once." Roger forked half the can into the milk bowl, covered the rest with plastic wrap, and put it in the refrigerator.

Roger watched the starving cat as he quickly emptied the bowl and stared up again.

"Nothing more for you until you're clean," Roger said as he plugged the kitchen sink and adjusted the tap water to warm. "I know what you're thinking, Tiger. As dirty as you are, I shouldn't give you a bath in the kitchen sink, of all places."

Tiger mewed softly.

"Well, it will take a lot of work to get this sink clean anyway. I'll tackle that next. So what if I begin with the sink dirtier than it was."

As the sink filled, Roger poured in some dishwashing detergent. It would have to do.

Into the sudsy water, Roger placed Tiger, who didn't even put up a fuss. "I thought you hated water," Roger mumbled in surprise. And it was almost as if Tiger purred in answer, *Not when compared to being filthy.*

After Tiger was rinsed off and the water was draining from the sink, Roger said, "Now, don't move until I get back."

Tiger was still standing, shivering in the sink when Roger returned with a towel. Soon one fluffy cat was damp-dry and purring gratefully.

"You're welcome," Roger said. "Would you like the rest of the tuna fish now?"

Roger spent the next hour cleaning the sink, washing and drying the dishes, and putting them away. He tidied the rest of the kitchen and by the time he was done, he had made two more trips to the garbage chute.

The apartment seemed to smell a little better so Roger closed the windows. He straightened the living room enough that he finally had a place to sit.

All of a sudden Roger hopped up. He wanted to see his old bedroom. He should have known better than to anticipate it being habitable. What hurt most was the thought that he *had* written to his parents two weeks ago not only to let them know he was coming but to give them time to prepare.

He would have emailed them, but a good old-fashioned letter with a stamp was more reliable when it came to people like his parents. If they had a computer and it was down, it would have most likely remained down. Besides, it didn't seem that his parents were the type to sift through dozens of junk emails, hoping to get one from their only child.

There was a bed in his old room, but it was covered with boxes and trash. Obviously, this had become the family junkyard after he moved out.

Roger returned to the couch and finished clearing it off. It would have to be his bed for the night. He sat down again, but was on his feet within a few minutes. He had decided to go shopping.

Chapter Five

AN OLD FRIEND

Roger stood on the narrow, concrete stoop just outside the tenement-house door. He snuggled momentarily in his coat as he considered which way to go. The decision made, he descended the snowy steps and turned right.

A block away, the first shops came into view. It was sad that so many storeowners had only halfheartedly decorated for Christmas. At most, some had hung a little tinsel and perhaps some garland across the three-foot wide door to their establishments.

Another half block and Roger saw a familiar little shop. It had been owned for as long as he could remember by the family of his only grade-school friend.

Just as Roger reached the store and placed his hand on the door, he remembered his friend's name: *Jerry— that was it. Scary Jerry we all called him. It was that scar he had across one cheek that had brought on the nickname.*

It never seemed to bother Jerry to have a nickname like that. And he spoke only once, that Roger could recall, of the time he was assaulted as a kid and was slashed across the face. Yet, he was the happiest, funniest boy Roger had ever known.

Jerry had always made a big deal of his nickname at Halloween time. He would dress up as a pirate or a soldier or corpse—anything to take advantage of the scar.

I wonder if I'll recognize his parents when I see them again, Roger thought as he entered and a small bell rang melodically. He needn't have worried. Jerry himself was behind the cash register.

"Good afternoon," Jerry said. "Is there something I can help you find?"

"You've moved things around," Roger said. "Where would I find air freshener?"

"I'll show you," Jerry offered as he slipped out from behind the counter. "It must be at least a year since you were in here. That's when my parents rearranged things."

Jerry handed Roger a can of Glade and asked, "Anything else?"

"I need cat food, paper towels, milk, bread, tuna fish,

salad dressing, lettuce, tomatoes, and some fruit. There must be a few more things. Yeah, how about some sliced cheese? That sounds good. I'll grab anything else I think of as I go along."

Jerry walked to the front of the shop and from next to the door he retrieved a miniature shopping cart.

Roger wondered if this incredible service was because no one else was in the store at the moment. Jerry seemed so happy that it couldn't possibly have mattered.

"You don't recognize me, do you Jerry?"

Jerry paused as he slowly placed a small bag of cat food into the cart. His eyebrows pursed and his natural smile was replaced by concentration. Then his face recaptured its happy glow. "Is that you Roger? My goodness, it can't be—can it?"

Roger reacted with a grin and several rapid nods. "It's me. How's Scary Jerry?"

"Not so scary anymore. I sort of grew out of that a few years ago—haven't been trick-or-treating recently at all."

"How are your mom and dad? I was expecting to see them in here when I set out this way."

The smile on Jerry's face disappeared.

"What's the matter, Jerry? I'm sorry if I brought up a bad subject," Roger said apologetically.

"Mom was killed in a holdup several months ago. And Dad, he drinks a lot more now. Sometimes I don't see him for a day or two at a time."

"I'm sorry, Jerry. I didn't know."

"How could you?" Jerry replied, sucking in his pain.

"I wish my parents had told me, but then...."

"Your dad was at the funeral, Roger. It was a nice service, but I miss my mom so much. I think she was the only one who ever really loved me."

"I am sorry, Jerry."

Jerry wiped something from his eyes in such a way that Roger felt he was to assume it was a loose eyelash or particle of dust.

Jerry took in a deep breath. "It is fortunate that high school was shortened to a three-year program. If it hadn't been, I don't know who would have taken over the store. You do remember when they made that change, don't you?"

"I certainly do," Roger said. "When it was first proposed, it had practically every high school student across the country up in arms."

"Who could blame them? None of them wanted to give up their senior year. Do you remember that too?"

"Yeah, and the solution was so simple," Roger added grinning.

"Things calmed right down when an eighth-grader suggested eliminating the freshman year of high school. No one ever enjoyed that first year, anyway," Jerry said.

"No freshman ever thought he'd live through it."

"Of course, that didn't make much difference to you and your plans. You finished high school when you were sixteen, if I remember right."

"You're right, Jerry. We sort of lost track of each other after I skipped the fifth and sixth grades," Roger pointed out.

Jerry shook his head. "I remember feeling abandoned, though it was no fault of yours that the school board felt they had to advance you to keep you challenged. We didn't see much of each other after that."

"I didn't see much of anybody after that, Jerry. I was placed in an intense, advanced science/math/engineering program for five very difficult and time-demanding years. There was little time for friends and no time for a social life. I never went to a prom or a play or even to a ball game."

"But it paid off, didn't it. Here you are. You're seventeen and almost through your second year at the most incredible technological university in the country."

"And yet I still have no social life."

"I bet you'd be surprised to learn that I applied to IPI a year ago. I hope to hear from them in time to matriculate this August—that is if I get accepted," Jerry said.

"I didn't know you were interested in automobiles and transportation," Roger said surprised.

"Of course you wouldn't. You suddenly shot two years ahead of me in school."

"It would be fun to see you around the campus this summer," Roger said.

"But that probably won't happen—you being two years ahead of me, and all."

"It could happen. In fact, I might be able to help it happen. I don't know if you realize how the five-year program works, but during a student's first two years, upperclassmen are assigned to assist them."

"That would be great fun, Roger, if I could work with you."

"Oh—I'm not sure how much fun that would be. The new students are worked pretty darn hard."

"I could handle it," Jerry said. Then the smile on his face faded as he glanced around the small store.

Roger sensed Jerry's feelings of entrapment. "You won't have to work here forever, will you?"

"I work here fourteen hours a day, seven days a week—even on Christmas Day. I can't see how my dad could ever run the store again. Wait, I take that back. A few weeks ago a ray of sunshine seemed to appear."

"What was that?"

"My dad was staggering the streets of Brooklyn one Sunday morning and literally stumbled into what appeared to be an apartment building."

"Appeared to be?" Roger asked.

"The ground floor turned out to be a church. Dad wandered in and slumped down on the back row. After the meeting everyone seemed to have somewhere else to go and left the chapel."

"Did your dad follow them?" Roger asked.

"Are you kidding? He just sat there, crocked plumb out of his mind."

Roger inhaled, ready to ask a question.

"Then this woman, a total stranger, sat down on the pew in front of him and turned around to face him. You won't believe this next part. She asked him if there was anything she could do to help."

"What did your dad say?"

"He rolled his eyes and belched."

Roger shook his head.

"Then a man slid in beside my dad and placed a hand on his shoulder. He helped my dad sit up straight and then got him talking."

"What did they talk about?" Roger asked.

"Whatever my dad felt like talking about. But that isn't what is most significant. This man and woman somehow made him feel like he still had something to live for. My dad hadn't felt that way since Mom died."

Jerry grew silent for a while.

"What happened next?"

"They talked for a couple of hours. Finally my dad decided to return to AA and to get sober, once and for all."

"If he pulls his life back together," Roger began, "he could run the store again. And that would make it possible for you to go on with your schooling, wouldn't it?"

"Yes, it would. But then it all depends on him pulling it together—and me being accepted into IPI."

"Try to be positive," Roger suggested.

Jerry shrugged. "They even talked a little bit about my situation. They *challenged* my dad to get ready to resume management of the store. It seems crazy that strangers would actually care about my dad, whom they had just met, and me whom they had never met."

"It does sound bizarre, especially for Brooklyn."

"But that isn't the strangest thing, Roger. This woman invited my dad to attend a meeting held the next evening. A dozen or so single people were there and my dad had a good time. They called it a family something-or-another. They are Mormons. Have you ever heard of Mormons before?"

"My roommate *is* one," Roger answered casually.

"Are they all really nice like these people?"

"I don't know about all of them, but I've met a few and they were okay. Your dad is very fortunate. Maybe he could get my dad to go with him to AA meetings."

"Wouldn't that be great?" Jerry said. "And if my dad starts pulling it together, maybe I *could* get him to invite your dad, and maybe your mom, to meet with these people."

Roger didn't say anything for a few minutes. He was wondering if there could actually be anyone in the world who might care enough to help *his* parents.

Jerry snapped Roger out of his reverie. "How is life at the big Institute?"

"It keeps me busy, that's for sure."

"I assume you came home to spend the holidays with your parents."

"That was the general idea. You see, I didn't come home for Christmas last year. I just couldn't make myself do it," Roger explained.

"Your dad still drinks a lot. Up until last weekend, mine and yours spent a lot of time together, doing just that."

"He wasn't home when I arrived a few hours ago. Neither was my mom. Do you know anything about her, Jerry?"

"She's about the same. She tried going through a withdrawal program a few months ago, but I heard she's punching the needle again."

"I guess that explains why neither of them was home." Roger closed his eyes, leaned his head back, and inhaled slowly. Then shaking his head just a little, he said, "I suppose Dad's out looking for a drink and Mom's out searching for a fix."

Roger found himself in front of the counter, unloading his purchases from the shopping cart. After the scanning was completed, Roger handed Jerry his credit card.

"This isn't an ordinary VISA or AMEX card, is it? Let me see. It says IPIS on it."

"It stands for International Polytechnic Institute Scholarship. My scholarship pays for more than tuition, books, and fees. It includes food, housing, a car, and spending money."

"Wow," Jerry said. "I wouldn't mind having one of those, but I didn't apply for a scholarship."

"Every student at IPI is on a completely paid scholarship," Roger said as he turned for the door, a shopping bag hanging from each hand.

"That's incredible. So, if I get accepted and find a way to attend, I won't have to lean on my dad or draw on my savings to finish school?"

"That's right. I do hope your dad gets his life under control, Jerry."

"Me, too. Will I see you again, Roger, before you go back to school?"

Roger paused before responding. He considered the approaching interaction with his parents. "I'll drop in, if I can."

Chapter Six

FATHER, MOTHER: FAREWELL

Roger proceeded back the way he had come with unsettling visions of seeing his parents for the first time in sixteen months.

For a brief dizzying moment, he experienced that uncomfortable feeling of déjà vu as he stood in front of the apartment building and gazed upward. Then, taking courage, he momentarily held both bags of groceries in one hand while he opened the front door and entered the foyer.

A quick glance at the mailboxes and Roger felt sure that at least one of his parents was at home. The corner of the letter that had been poking out of the side of the mailbox was gone.

Once again Roger climbed the stairs. He paused and inhaled deeply before knocking on the door to his parents' apartment.

He listened carefully, but heard nothing. He knocked a little louder to no avail. Finally, Roger knocked loudly.

There was a shuffle inside followed by the sound of breaking glass and muffled profanity. Roger cringed at what must have just happened.

Then he waited—and waited. He set the two plastic bags down. Only then did he notice how the thin handles had been cutting into his tense fingers.

After what sounded like scratching on the other side of the door, Roger heard a mumbled slur of two words, "Who's there?"

"Roger."

Something bumped and then brushed against the inside of the door. After what seemed an eternity to Roger and following a click, the door opened with a slight jerk. One squinting eye of a wrinkled, unshaven face peered through a two-inch crack in the doorway. "Is that really you, Roger?" it said haltingly.

"It's me Dad. I came to spend Christmas with you and Mom."

"Christmas?"

"Yes, Christmas," Roger said as if providing new information to his father. Perhaps he was.

Then suddenly the door jerked open. "What the hell are you doing here, Roger?"

Roger entered. Once again the rank smell of tobacco and booze filled the room. And there, next to the couch was a broken bottle, its contents puddled on the floor.

Roger's father closed the door and turned toward the couch.

"Stop, Dad!" Roger warned. "Wait until I clean up the broken glass."

Roger's dad leaned unsteadily back against the door.

Roger hurried into the kitchen, placed the shopping bags on the counter, and returned with a broom, dust pan, and an old dishcloth.

His father staggered forward.

"Dad, let me help you," Roger said and led his father to a worn-out swivel rocker.

"Where's my glass?" he mumbled.

Roger glanced over at the sofa table. In the bottom of a tumbler were a couple swallows-worth of redeye. He handed the glass to his dad and turned around to clean up the spill.

"Where's Mom?" Roger asked pleasantly.

"Huh? Oh, I don't know."

"Do you have any idea when she'll be home?" Roger asked.

"How would I know that?" his father replied curtly. "Didn't I just tell you I don't even know *where* she is?"

Roger swept up the last of the broken glass, soaked up the spilled booze, picked up the cleaning supplies, and returned to the kitchen. After dumping the glass into the trash can and rinsing out the dishcloth, he washed his hands and put the groceries away.

At the sound of the refrigerator door opening, Tiger emerged from a far corner of the kitchen. He rubbed against Roger's leg. "Be patient, Tiger. I haven't forgotten you."

Tiger mewed affectionately.

When Roger reentered the living room, his father was slumped to one side and breathing lightly. His right arm was hanging along the side of the chair and an empty glass was lying on the floor, not far away. Roger picked it up and took it to the kitchen.

Before he had time to return, he heard a jiggling sound at the front door. After a long pause the doorknob rattled. Roger crossed the room and cautiously opened the door.

There was his mother—one arm draped loosely around the neck of a woman Roger vaguely recognized. She had her right arm around his mother's waist.

Roger's glassy-eyed mother didn't even acknowledge him. "Let me help you...," he began as he addressed the stranger.

"Lydia. My name is Lydia," the woman uttered haltingly. She appeared spaced out as well.

"Thank you for helping Mom up the stairs. It was kind of you," Roger said as he situated his mother on the couch.

"You're Roger, aren't you?" Lydia slurred as she swayed just inside the door. "I remember you."

Roger smiled.

"I'm sorry about your mom. I was so sure we could find her a fix somewhere. But even between us, we didn't have enough money."

"I heard she was in rehab not long ago," Roger said.

"We both were," Lydia mumbled, her words a barely coherent mumble. "It didn't work out; maybe some other day."

Roger followed her out the door and onto the landing where Lydia had floundered forward and was gripping the banister.

"Would you like some help down the stairs?" Roger asked.

Lydia looked over the rail and her head swooned.

Roger glanced at his parents. Both were passed out. He closed the front door and gently took Lydia's arm. Ever so slowly they made their way down the steps.

At the fourth-floor landing, Roger guided Lydia toward the next flight of steps. She resisted.

Nodding to the right, she said, "This is my apartment."

Roger held on to the woman while she rummaged through her purse and finally found a key her trembling hand repeatedly failed to insert into the lock. Roger took the key and unlocked the door. After making sure she was seated comfortably on her couch, he asked, "You'll be okay?"

"Sure."

"Is there anything I can do for you? 'Fix you something to eat?"

Lydia wrapped her arms around herself. "Could you hand me that blanket—the one over there on the floor? I'm so cold."

Roger climbed the stairs and stepped back into his parents' apartment. Both were sleeping.

Roger returned to the kitchen and searched the cupboards. He found two cans of tomato soup. After filling Tiger's bowl with cat food, he put a saucepan and a skillet on the stove and began fixing a simple dinner.

Tomato soup and grilled cheese sandwiches had long been one of Roger's favorite lunches. That was back before his mother met Lydia and they became close *friends*. Since that time, he had pretty much cooked for himself.

Roger cleaned the debris off a small table that was pushed up loosely against the outside wall of the small kitchen.

He found a crumpled up tablecloth stuffed in the back of a cabinet drawer. Roger pulled the trash can out from beneath the sink and did his best to funnel the tablecloth's crumbs into it. He would sweep the floor later.

He threw the cloth across the table, making sure the heaviest stains were against the wall. After he set the table, he went into the living room and nudged his parents.

Neither of them moved, except to breath.

Roger ate dinner alone, glancing from time to time

into the living room. He cleaned the kitchen, but left the unused bowls, plates, and spoons in place.

He stared out the small kitchen window. It was getting dark outside. Of course, it never was very light in the tight space between his parents' apartment building and the next one, especially during winter.

There were clothes hanging on several lines that stretched between adjacent buildings. Somebody, one level below and across the alley threw open her kitchen window and began reeling in her family's frost–covered clothing. There were no men's clothes—just a woman's and what looked like those for a baby and a toddler.

"If it isn't booze or drugs, it's abandonment or divorce," Roger muttered to no one in particular.

He looked into the living room again. His parents were still out cold. He had anticipated sleeping on the couch, but it was occupied. A second look in his old bedroom and Roger decided to roll up his sleeves once again and tackle the job of making another room habitable.

Several empty whiskey and vodka boxes cluttered the top of his bed.

"Oh how I wish these had arrived here empty," Roger said to Tiger who slinked into the room. "Could they have been full of groceries when they came into the apartment?"

Tiger mewed as if answering.

"I should have thought of that, Tiger," Roger said. "No way could my dad have afforded to buy a whole case of booze at any one time. Thank heavens for that."

Tiger mewed again as though agreeing.

With the boxes and clutter off the bed, Roger straightened the soiled bedspread. As he entered the living room to get his suitcase, he saw his father sitting up in his chair.

"Where's that bottle?" he demanded. "What did you do with it, Roger?"

"It's in the trash…," Roger began.

"You had no right to throw it away!"

"I didn't throw…," Roger said.

"Liar!" Roger's father yelled as he tried to rise, teetered a bit, and fell back into the chair. "Go get it, damn you!"

"Dad," Roger said. "Take it easy. Please."

"I mean it, Roger. Just go get it," he said pleadingly. "I'll feel better if I can just have a little drink."

"Don't you remember? You dropped the bottle on the floor. I wiped up the spill and swept up the broken glass."

Roger's father raked the fingers of both hands through his thinning hair, his eyes squinted closed. "I remember now," he said. "The bottle fell out of my hand when you pounded on the door. You made me drop it, Roger!"

"I'm sorry, Dad."

"Go get me another one!" he demanded.

"You know that stuff is rotting your insides. Your liver can't keep up forever with all the alcohol you keep pouring into your stomach."

"I said go get me another bottle, Roger. And I mean it!"

Roger touched his father gently on the arm, but his father jerked away.

"Go get me another bottle, Roger!" Then his demeanor softened. "Please. I promise when I finish the next bottle, I'll never touch another drop as long as I live. That's a promise, son."

Roger stepped back. "I can't do it, Dad."

The rage returned. "I'm still your father! And until you're an adult, you'll do what I tell you to do!"

"Dad," Roger said gently. "The fact that I'm still a minor is one reason I can't get you a fresh bottle."

"I'll call down to the liquor store and okay it for you."

"It's still illegal, Dad."

"I know Fred down there. He won't tell."

"No, Dad."

Roger's father staggered to his feet and yelled, "Then get out of here!"

Roger's mother jerked at her husband's outburst, but never opened her eyes.

While Roger's father staggered toward the front door, Roger picked up his attaché case, opened it, and removed two wrapped Christmas gifts. These he placed on the small table next to the chair his father had just vacated.

Roger paused next to his sleeping mother and tenderly touched her cheek with the side of one of his fingers. He leaned over and kissed her forehead.

Then, with the front door open, Roger picked up his small suitcase and walked out onto the landing. He turned and for just a moment he looked back inside. With loving eyes he considered his mother. If only he had been able to say goodbye to her in a way she would remember.

His father had his head down as if to emphasize that any further discussion was useless. Before Roger had crossed the landing the door slammed behind him. Slowly, Roger descended the stairs.

When he reached the main floor, he saw someone outside attaching a piece of paper to one of the few unbroken panes of glass in the front-door window. Roger opened the door and read what it said.

ATTENTION: Occupants of this building are hereby notified that demolition of this building will commence 60 days hence and therefore said building is to be vacated 30 days hence.

You are hereby notified that you must relocate within the above stated time frame.

signed: Carmichael Demolition, Inc. on behalf of Brooklyn Redevelopment

"And you chose Christmas Day to inform these people?" Roger said bitterly.

The man who had just posted the notice turned

around and stared at Roger with a blank expression. "Would tomorrow have been any better?" Then he walked away.

"Probably not," Roger said sadly to himself as he turned the other way and began a slow walk to the subway.

Chapter Seven

ROOMMATES: BOUND FOR MICHIGAN

The route to the subway passed within a block of the store where Jerry worked. Roger decided to stop in.

An old fashioned bell chimed as the door opened. Once again, the shop was empty except for Jerry, who was sweeping the floor near the back. At the first sound of the bell, Jerry stopped what he was doing and searched for his customer.

"Oh, hi, Roger," he said as happy as ever. "What can I get you this time?"

Roger set his suitcase and attaché case next to the small shopping carts. He said, "I've decided to head back to school."

"I was afraid you might not stay very long."

Roger gazed around as if he had actually entered the store intent on making a purchase.

"Did you and your dad argue?" Jerry asked.

"Not really. He got mad at me, though. He accused me of throwing away a bottle of booze when in reality he dropped and broke it himself. He was so drunk."

Roger selected a package of Twinkies and a chug of chocolate milk. He held them up apologetically and said, "I picked up this habit from my roommate at school. Good ole Blake—eat junk food when you're feeling down."

Jerry slid the items across the scanner. A bell dinged after detecting each item and the purchase price appeared on a screen. Roger glanced at the sales slip. The computer had recognized his voice and had retrieved his IPIS card number.

"I'd like to ask a special favor from you."

"What is it, Roger?"

"The building where my parents live is scheduled to be demolished in two months. My mom and dad have thirty days to get out."

"Oh, I'm so sorry. What are they going to do?"

Roger shook his head. "They don't even know the building is coming down. The notice was posted just a few minutes ago, on Christmas Day, if you can believe it.

"My dad and I may not have argued, Jerry, but we didn't separate on the best of terms. He demanded that I buy him a new bottle of booze. I'm a minor and I'm sure I'd lose my scholarship if I was caught purchasing liquor. My entire future would probably go down the drain."

Jerry said sadly, "And that rotgut wouldn't have helped him any either. How was your mom?"

"She was stoned out of her head the entire time I was there. She'll never know I came home for Christmas, except for a gift I left for her. I hope my dad doesn't throw it away before she sees it."

"That must be the most difficult thing about leaving so soon," Jerry said sympathetically.

"It is, but I had to go."

"Would you like me to check on them from time to time?"

Roger nodded. "Yes, that's the favor I need—*if* you can find out where they move to." Then he slipped the bag of goodies into his suitcase.

"I'm glad you dropped by," Jerry said as he accepted a small card from Roger. "Nice business card—IPI logo and all. I *will* let you know what happens with your parents."

"Thanks, Jerry. Good luck with the store and getting into IPI. I'd love to see you around campus next summer."

Roger could never remember walking to Line F nor the transfer at West 4th Street to Line A. He vaguely recalled getting off at Washington Heights and the short walk to the parking tower where he had left his car.

He removed the Locator pendant from his key ring and pressed his thumb into the small pad in its center. A cheerful female voice responded.

"Roger, you are standing at the entrance to the Washington Heights Parking Tower."

"I know that," Roger said a little ruffled.

"Of course you do," she said without emotion. "As a courtesy reminder, your car is on level fourteen, parking stall G27. Once you arrive on that level, you will be given further instructions"

Roger entered the structure and stepped onto a moving sidewalk. Usually he would have walked beside it, but he was preoccupied, thinking about the encounter he had had with his father. That he hadn't been able to speak with his mother added to the distraction.

At the end of the moving walkway, he stepped off in front of an elevator. The ride up took a matter of seconds. As the doors opened, Roger heard, "Proceed carefully. Watch for moving vehicles. Walk straight ahead five rows and turn right. Your car is the seventh one on the left."

"Thank you," Roger said. Then under his breath he added. "One day my car will be delivered to me at street level."

The feminine voice of the garage hostess continued. "That convenience will be available in seven months, two weeks, and three work days. A new parking tower is under construction just across the street. Then, this parking tower will be razed. I only have one question, Roger. Will I dream?"

"You've downloaded too many old movies," Roger remarked indifferently to the computer-generated voice. Just ahead, he saw his car. As he approached, the door opened.

"How was your visit?" Phi asked. "Are you still glad that you didn't take me along?"

Roger thought for a moment. "I believe it was best you weren't there."

"Things must have transpired as you anticipated."

"Not exactly. They were worse."

"I had a hunch that that was the case when you returned so soon. You had thought to at least spend the night."

"What a silly notion," said Roger. After a short pause, he added," I don't want to talk about it right now. Just get us to I-80 and on our way back to school. Okay?"

"Sure," Phi said as he backed the car out and began the spiraling trip down to ground level. The driver's window lowered as the car stopped at the kiosk. Roger reached out and dropped the Locator into a small return chute. Then he swiped his IPIS credit/ID card through the designated slot.

"Have a nice trip back to Brighton and good luck with your next quarter of school," the female voice said cheerfully.

"I will," Roger responded. "And may you happily serve many two-legged and four-wheeled patrons of this lovely parking tower, as long as it shall stand."

"I shall surely try," the voice responded solemnly.

Phi maneuvered the car onto the street and headed for the Washington Toll Bridge.

"As soon as we leave I-95 and are on I-80 I will take us up to the speed limit. Then it is a simple non-stop, three-and-a-half hour drive to Brighton, Michigan."

"That suits me fine."

"Roger, I just checked your vital signs. Your visit must have upset you more than I sensed when you got in the car."

"I'll be okay, Phi."

"If you would like to sleep, I can recline the back of your seat, activate the massage function, and provide some soothing music.

Roger exhaled a controlled slow breath as he began to relax. "That would be wonderful," he said.

As his eyes closed he felt the gradual acceleration of the car and the slightly higher pitch of its motor.

At Des Moines, Psi stopped the car at the recharging island at a Power-Up Mart not far off the freeway. Blake stirred and opened his eyes. Psi returned Blake's seat to the upright position.

"I thought you might want to get out and stretch a bit," Psi said.

Blake clambered out of the car without his coat and hurried to the kiosk. Inside, he first visited the Men's room. Then, after pausing in front of the candy counter, he wandered farther into the store.

He finally stopped at the sandwich and salad bar, but the thought of cold food trapped in plastic wrap was not appealing. In the end, Blake selected two cups of hot chili, a box of Ritz crackers, and a small bottle of antacid tablets.

Back inside the car, Blake shivered. The chili would hit the spot. As he began to eat, he watched the city lights pass by outside his window.

Not long after Psi had the car back on I-80 he gradually increased its speed to the 180-mph speed limit.

Blake finished the first cup of chili and put the second one in the refrigerator. The chili had been spiced hotter than he had anticipated and although the Ritz crackers had neutralized it a little, Blake found himself saying, "Thank heavens for the antacid tablets."

Then Psi brought the video monitor to life. As Blake leaned back, a Disney/Pixar short began to play on the screen. He had missed the title, but he knew this one by heart: a large bird perches on a sagging telephone wire with several small birds at each side. The small birds laugh and make fun of their visitor and eventually peck at his toes after he has fallen upside down and continues to hold on. Near the end, the large bird lets go and the small birds shoot into the sky, leaving their feathers behind. The large bird has the last laugh.

Blake laughed too. Though the short was decades old, he always found it amusing.

Psi kept Blake entertained for half hour or so with other Disney shorts. Finally, in keeping with the season, he played an animated feature-length film entitled *Tivoli's Christmas.*

As this movie ended, Psi said, "You are falling asleep, Blake."

"I don't know if it was the food or the stress of this morning, but yes, I won't be awake much longer."

"Let me make you comfortable," Psi offered.

With his seat reclined, the massage mechanism going, and another Chopin nocturne playing softly, Blake soon fell asleep.

When Blake awoke, he felt as though he had hardly slept a wink. He sat up and looked around. Immediately Blake recognized where he was. They had decelerated in anticipation of the off-ramp nearest the IPI campus.

"You slept for two hours, Blake," Psi said. "I hope you didn't mind me not waking you."

Blake rubbed his eyes. "No, I must have needed the sleep. In fact, thanks for helping the last part of the trip go by so quickly."

Psi directed the car to the central campus parking tower. Parking for cars assigned to undergraduate students was restricted to the upper four levels.

Blake glanced at the northeast corner of the residential tower, which stood a hundred or so feet to the south. He spotted the windows to his suite, eight stories up.

The windows were dark—the entire building and the ones on either side were pitch-black inside as well.

"I must be the only living soul on campus," Blake said.

Psi responded immediately. "Actually, you aren't. There are seventeen security personnel and half a dozen maintenance workers scattered around the campus. Wait just a minute."

"Why?" Blake asked.

"Just a moment. There, I notified the Security Center computer that you have returned to campus early and will be occupying your apartment for the rest of the holiday break. She wishes you an enjoyable time, lonely though it may be."

"Tell her thanks," Blake said indifferently.

"I already did."

After Psi parked the car in Blake's assigned space, the driver's door opened. Blake climbed out with a bag of uneaten food in one hand and his coat slung over his arm. The instant the door closed, the trunk lid popped up. Blake retrieved the suitcase he hadn't bothered to take into the house the previous day and headed for the elevator.

Inside the multi-directional elevator, Blake sensed its motion downward, then laterally to the south, and back up into the dormitory tower. The door opened at the eighth floor and the overhead lights down the left hallway lighted. After Blake reached the end of the corridor, lights in the ceiling of the hall to the right came on and the ones behind him turned off.

At the end of the second hall was the door to the suite he shared with Roger. All of a sudden light shot brightly from beneath his apartment door. Blake's heart leaped.

"I'm sorry, Blake. I keep forgetting things like that startle you."

"Very cute, Psi. I know you were fully aware that I anticipated the apartment being dark. You flicked on the lights just as you noticed me looking at the bottom of the door."

"You caught me, Blake. I thought it would be a fine joke. You were surprised, weren't you?"

"Yes, Psi. And it was a very fine joke."

"I activated climate control the moment we entered the campus. You will find it nice and cozy inside. There is even some easy listening music playing in the living room. Is there anything else you would like me to do?"

"Is there a tub of hot water waiting in the bathroom?" Blake asked.

"There would be if I thought you intended to take a bath. There is plenty of hot water for a shower, though."

"Yes, that's what I need, a hot shower and a warm bed."

"I'll have your bed heated to your liking by the time you are finished with your shower."

"That sounds great, Psi."

Chapter Eight

MIDNIGHT SCARE

Blake donned a terry cloth bathrobe, stood in front of the mirror, and toweled his hair dry.

"Your bed is at your preferred temperature, Blake. I'd turn the covers down for you if I could," Psi said pleasantly.

"I know you would. Maybe one year I'll make a robotic body for you. Then you could actually do things like that."

"I wouldn't have to wait that long if Roger took on the task. If he put his mind to it, he could pull it off in less than a week."

"During the foreseeable future, he won't have time,

Psi. I can guarantee that," Blake said.

"Oh, I know," Psi responded disappointedly. "You both have that huge project you must complete by the end of your second year of school. Moving on into your third year depends on it."

Blake walked casually into the living room. He melted into a soft leather chair, picked up the book he had left half-read just before leaving for home.

He noted the penciled tick mark he had made in the margin and continued reading from there. Soon he was completely lost in the fascinating in-depth message of the book. He had read it several times before and each time he had found *Biochip Fundamentals* the most interesting book he had ever read.

But intriguing or not, Blake soon began to doze.

"Your bed is still as you like it, Blake. Perhaps this would be a good time to retire for the day."

Blake got up, stretched, and made his way to his bedroom. The bed was perfectly comfortable and Blake fell asleep before the first dozen measures of Debussy's *Clouds* had played.

After the music stopped, complete stillness pervaded Blake's room and the entire suite. The unsettling quiet affected Blake's efforts to sleep and he began to toss and turn.

Sometime around midnight he awoke to absolute silence, which seemed about to smoother him. All of a sudden Blake bolted upright, and for a few moments he perched on the edge of his bed, shaking. As he began to relax, he squinted at the grayish objects in his unlighted room.

All of a sudden Blake lurched. His breathing and heartbeat raced each other again. He had heard a noise in the living room just before light had abruptly appeared beneath his bedroom door.

"Calm down," Psi suggested casually. "There is nothing to be afraid of. You know I would have warned you if there was. Think. What is the most likely origin of sudden light in the living room?"

Blake leaped up and yanked opened the door. "Roger, what in the world are you doing here?"

Roger stumbled back. "Might I ask the same about you?"

Blake turned and flopped down on a nearby chair. "Things didn't go so well with my dad."

"That would have been my first guess," Roger said after regaining his composure. "You had misgivings about going home in the first place."

"So did you. I assume things didn't work out with your family either."

Roger shook his head as he walked past Blake and into his own bedroom. "No, things did not work out."

"I'm sorry," Blake said. "How are your parents?"

"Not good. You see, I bumped into an old grade-school friend. He said my mom had been in rehab at one time, but recently she'd gone back to needles and the hard stuff."

"I am sorry," Blake said again.

"And he told me my dad might begin going to AA meetings, but that is yet to be seen." Roger reentered the living room and sat across from Blake. "So, what happened with your dad and his determination that you become a missionary?"

"He was pushy as usual. I wish he could understand that the harder he pushes, the harder I resist."

"Hey, there's some good insight into yourself."

"Oh, I know I can be stubborn. I probably got it from him. But he's older and should be wiser and more flexible."

Roger shook his head. "So much for self-insight. Some day you ought to ponder that last statement, Blake. You just might find a flaw somewhere in your reasoning."

"I can already see it. I saw it before I said it, but at that moment I didn't care," Blake said. Then he added, "I still don't."

Blake followed his roommate into the kitchen where Roger opened the refrigerator and looked inside. It was practically empty and so was the freezer. The cupboards were sparsely stocked as well.

"I'm going to take a shower," Roger said. "I slept most of the way back to Brighton. After I'm done, let's take a trip to Kroger's."

"I'll get dressed while you clean up."

Twenty-five minutes later, Roger emerged from his

bedroom. Blake was sitting on the sofa with *Biochip Fundamentals* propped up in his lap.

Roger leaned over and tipped the book forward so he could see the title. "Engrossing stuff, right?"

"Absolutely. Oh, you're making fun, aren't you? Well, I'll remember that next time I can't tear you away from one of your books on thermodynamics or electromagnetic linkage."

"You do that, Blake. Ready to go?"

Blake leaped up, slipped into his bedroom, and returned as he stuffed his wallet into a back pocket.

As the roommates left the parking-tower elevator, Roger said, "Let's take my car. It's a little closer."

Fifteen minutes later, Phi directed the car off East Grand River Avenue and south into Kroger's parking lot.

Roger removed two canvas shopping bags from behind the driver's seat. Before he could close the door, Phi said, "You'll need at least two more bags if you intend to restock your refrigerator, freezer, and cupboards."

Roger looked at Blake who shrugged. "We might as well. It'll save a trip back next week."

"Now that that's settled," Psi said, "does it matter which of you is going to get fresh food and which is going to get dry goods?"

"It doesn't matter to me," Blake said.

"Me either," Roger added.

Psi said to Phi, "You got dry goods last time. Let's simply switch."

"Now that that's settled," Phi said, "I'll race you to check out, Psi."

Blake slipped his super smart phone into the slot on the front of his shopping cart. On the video screen just beyond the carts handle, a list of the needed dry goods appeared. "Try to keep up," Psi said to Blake as he started the cart's servomechanisms. "As you might have guessed, I have plotted the most efficient way to get everything. Phi's course is going to take 14 seconds fewer than ours, unless I can shave off some time."

"Psi, this is not a race," Blake stated pitifully.

"Perhaps not to you, but to Phi and me, well, it is one of our few pleasures. You wouldn't deny us a little amusement, would you?" Psi pleaded pathetically.

Blake said, "Okay. I would hate to see a super smart phone cry."

The cart jolted ahead, moving faster than usual.

"Get ready, now, Blake," Psi warned. "Fourteen point six feet ahead on the right is the canned soup. Grab six cans of tomato, four of chicken noodle, and one each of cream of chicken and cream of mushroom. And be quick about it."

Blake shook his head as he mumbled, "This is ridiculous."

"Keep your disparaging remarks to yourself, please."

"Why? You've probably reprogrammed yourself by now to read my mind."

Psi didn't respond, which was quite out of the ordinary.

Blake actually began to wonder. "You can't read my mind, can you?" Blake asked beseechingly.

"Get ready again," Psi called out. "Sixteen point three feet ahead on the left is the cereal. I'm only going to stop for 3.4 seconds. If you haven't got everything by then, you'll have to run to catch up.

"Grab one box each of Honey Nut Cheerios and Honey Bunches of Oats with almonds. Then grab two boxes of Lucky Charms."

Blake was too slow and ended up chasing after Psi and the cart with the last two boxes of cereal. "Why did we get Lucky Charms? Roger and I have never bought them before."

"Oh, that. It was Phi's and my idea. We figured you needed all the luck you could get with your project."

"What?" Blake asked.

"A joke? You know, as Spock said, 'A story with a humorous climax.'"

Blake remained stone-faced.

"Star Trek IV? Never mind. Three point one feet on your left: select one 16-ounce bag each of the following frozen items: corn, peas, green beans, mixed vegetables, and broccoli-cauliflower. I can't believe you don't remember Spock saying that."

"Spock never said that, Psi. Leonard Nimoy did."

Psi responded with, "Coming up eight point seven feet on your left, get ready to grab: a one-pound bag of spaghetti and a 16-ounce jar of Ragu sauce."

Blake began breathing heavily. Psi noticed. "Stay with me just a little longer. We have one minute and twelve seconds to go. And more importantly, we're three seconds ahead of Phi and Roger."

In the end, the race was a tie. Both carts arrived at adjacent checkout stands, simultaneously. As the carts rolled beneath overhead scanners, a charming female voice said, "Hello, Blake and Roger. Did you find everything you wanted?"

Psi and Phi answered loudly and in unison, "Yes, we did."

"Oh, I apologize for bypassing the two of you. How do you want to divide up the items for payment?"

Psi said, "Blake? Roger?"

Blake replied, "Just charge half of the total to each of our accounts."

"That's all right with me," Roger added.

The boys loaded the grocery bags into the trunk and climbed into the car.

Roger asked, "Did you get anything that might thaw in the next half hour?"

"Just some frozen vegetables, but they're in an insulated bag. Besides, if you're concerned about them thawing, they're in the trunk and it's freezing in there."

"How about dropping in at Patti's Pastry Palace?" Roger suggested. "I'm not sleepy."

Blake and Roger sat near the front of the shop. Blake had two chocolate covered Pershings and an extra-large Styrofoam cup of hot chocolate in front of him. Roger faced a bagel and a small carton of 1% milk.

"Roger, did you know that Psi and Phi have senses of humor?"

"No. Did you program them to?"

"Not a chance! But it appears their biochip-generated intelligence is becoming more sentient than I would have ever imagined."

Psi said, "Just listen to them, Phi. They're talking as if we weren't even here."

"How rude," Phi added, an insulted lilt to his voice.

"Sorry, guys," Blake said. "This is going to take some getting used to."

Roger said, "So what makes you think they have senses of humor?"

"They had me grab two boxes of Lucky Charms. They figured we'd need a huge helping of luck with regards to our sophomore project."

"They may be right," Roger said. "Let's talk about that for a few minutes. As for you, Phi and Psi, feel free to listen in. We just might need your input."

Chapter Nine

A BRAINSTORMING SESSION

Blake asked, "Did you have time during break to think about our project?"

"Not really. I had planned to before leaving for Brooklyn, but the stress of going home stifled any creativity. In the end I simply watched a couple of movies."

"Which ones?" Psi asked.

"Oh, I watched Star Trek XXVI, for one, and…."

Psi interrupted, "Do you remember Star Trek IV? That's the one in which Spock defines a joke as 'a story with a humorous climax,' right?"

"Yeah," Phi said. "It's when Spock has that crazy

conversation with Dr. McCoy."

"That's enough, you two," Blake said, "Someday I may get used to your newfound senses of humor. But if you get too carried away, I promise I'll reprogram each of you to be just like Data."

"Hah!" Psi said. "I know you like me just the way I am *and* you know I know it."

Blake turned to Roger. "I hope Phi isn't a pain in the neck."

"So far, so good," Roger replied. "Now, if two small computers could be quiet for awhile, Blake and I have some important things to discuss."

"You said you might need our input and insight, didn't you?" Psi asked.

"Regarding our project, Phi; not about just any old thing."

"Oh. I'll hush up," Psi said contritely.

"How about you, Blake. Did you have any ideas for a project? We must have one that will knock the socks off not only the project administrators but the entire faculty."

"And student body!" Psi added.

"And your pocket-pal computers!" Phi said merrily.

"Hush, you two!" Blake demanded. After a moment of ensuing silence, Blake continued. "I did have an interesting thought Christmas Eve," Blake began. "I should have been dozing off so Santa would be sure to drop by...."

"Come on," Psi said. "Even I don't believe in Santa."

Phi added, "I don't believe in him any more either."

"Please, you two," Blake said with firmness.

Psi went on. "Do you mean to say that you believed in Santa Claus at one time?"

"Just pipe down, okay?"

"Well, a...actually...," Phi stammered.

"If you haven't anything constructive to say, just be quiet," Blake stated with a tone of finality.

Blake waited for a reply but didn't get one. "I could just switch you off, you know."

Psi and Phi giggled softly.

Blake rolled his eyes as he turned away from the two electronic clowns. Facing Roger, he said. "Something strange, yet exciting, popped into my mind two nights ago."

"What was that?" Roger asked.

"You know how they say the universe exists as an expanding bubble—that all matter is located on and within this film?"

"That idea has mostly been discarded," Roger said.

"But, if it were true, then, nothing at all exists inside the bubble."

Roger nodded pensively.

"So, if there is absolutely nothing within the bubble, the spherical inside has no dimensions. And if there are no linear dimensions inside, it would take zero time to travel from any one point on the inner bubble surface to any other point on that surface."

Roger rubbed his chin and closed his eyes.

"What do you think?"

"It's a bit bizarre, but I'll give it some thought," Roger said as he gathered his empty carton and napkins, stood up, and headed for the exit. He dropped his stuff into the trash receptacle and pushed his way through the door.

Suddenly Roger playfully shoved his roommate. "Way to go, Blake! You may have something there. The more I think about your idea, the more I like it. So why were you holding back?"

"What do you mean?" Blake asked.

"You know! Aren't you suggesting we build a car that can take us clear across the universe in the blink of an eye?"

Blake did not respond. That thought had never occurred to him.

The following day, Blake woke up midmorning. He could hear clicking in Roger's room. Pulling on his bathrobe, Blake left his bedroom and tapped lightly on Roger's door, which was open a few inches.

"Roger," Blake whispered to his roommate, who was hunched over his computer and tapping away furiously. "Roger," he said a little louder.

"Huh? Oh, good morning Blake. I'll have you know your idea cost me a night's sleep. I hope you appreciate that."

"So the idea is okay?"

"Yeah, it's more than okay. Come on in and sit

down," Roger said, motioning to the chair at the foot of his bed.

"How far have you got with the idea?" Blake asked.

"I have a feeling—a theory, actually—that what you hit on is not only valid, but right on the money. I'm on the verge of figuring out how it works."

Blake sat down. "And?"

"Let me assure you that *if* there is nothing inside the bubble, not even empty space, there is indeed no distance between any two points on the bubble's inner surface—just as you suggested—hence, travel time between any two points on this spherical inner surface is zero!"

"It sounded so simple," Blake said, "when it first came to me."

"The concept itself is simple, but beyond that, it is quite complex. You see, the way I just explained it, the entire inner surface could actually be defined as a point. Now, I need to get back to work."

"Would you like to stop for breakfast? I'll prepare it."

Roger glanced at the bottom right-hand corner of his computer screen. "How about lunch, sleepy head?"

"How about brunch?" Blake countered.

"Okay," Roger replied. "I'd like my usual: fried egg on toast. And, today, for a change, rather than apple-cinnamon oatmeal, I'll have a huge bowl of those Lucky Charms—not because I need luck but because I'm already having it."

Blake could hear Psi snickering back in his room. Phi

was laughing on Roger's desk.

All of a sudden, Roger ran into the kitchen, his hands holding the sides of his head. "I've got to get to the Lab."

"The Lab Building must be closed for the holidays, Roger. We won't be able to get in for at least a week."

Roger shook his head as he slipped his wallet and keys into his pockets. "I'll get in somehow."

"I'll wait here for you," Blake said. "I'm hungry and breakfast sounds pretty good to me."

"Sorry, Blake, you've got to come with me. This project was your idea in the first place. Get Psi while I grab Phi. It's going to take all four of us."

One glance at the look on Roger's face and Blake turned off the stove and grabbed his keys, wallet, and coat.

Roger pulled on his coat as he shot out of the apartment door and darted toward the elevator.

Roger leaped out of the car and ran toward the cylindrical Security Center building, over which cantilevered a huge geodesic-dome skylight. The front door was unlocked, though no one seemed to be around.

Blake caught up with Roger at the front desk.

"May I help you?" a feminine computer voice asked.

"We need to do some important research in the Lab," Roger said.

"One moment please," the computer responded—then

paused a few seconds. "You're Roger—and you're Blake."

"And I'm Psi. Meet my friend Phi."

The computer replied, "Very good bio-engineering, Blake. I'm KDO. Most students call me Kiddo. Now, let me explain a little bit about Lab-use during holidays. Unlimited student access to Laboratory facilities is a privilege offered only to the academic top ten percent of second-year seniors—that's fifth-year students."

"I know that," Roger said. "But it is imperative that I have access to the Lab and the school's computers while I still have certain ideas and concepts in my head."

"And," Kiddo continued without a change of voice inflection, "there are no exceptions."

Roger inhaled deeply, as if preparing for a verbal battle.

"Hold on to that breath, Roger. I am just now receiving your and Blake's annotated grade reports for last quarter. Hmm. Really?"

"What?" Roger demanded impatiently.

"It seems that there are two exceptions, namely, you and Blake. So, you really got an A+ in Automotive Thermodynamics VI and Intra-molecular Linkage V? And you, Blake got an A+ in both Artificial Intelligence VII and Advanced Biochip Engineering VI? And, oh my goodness, you both got A's in each of your other classes. It appears that you are the only undergraduate students with a key to the campus, so to speak. You know where to go, I presume."

"You presume correctly," Roger said as he shoved himself free of the counter and hurried back toward the front door.

With everyone in the car, Phi backed it out of the parking space and sped toward the Ford-Tesla-Edison Laboratory Building, which was located across campus.

Kiddo hadn't been joking about Roger and Blake having total access to the Laboratory Building.

As the two boys approached the front door, one exterior and one interior foyer light switched on. The handicap doors opened automatically. Once inside, the exterior light flicked off and a light down the main corridor came on.

Lights came on in front of and turned off behind Blake and Roger as they rushed through the building. They started down the hall leading to the labs, but no lights came on to lead that way. Instead, a light illuminated the first part of the corridor leading into the upperclassmen block of offices.

Blake and Roger stopped short. After exchanging a brief glance of puzzlement with each other, they shrugged and followed the lights to where only one remained on—in front of an office door. Two name plaques, attached to the door, read: **Blake Stevens** and **Roger Greggson**.

There was an unexpected click and the door to the office opened. The lights flicked on. Roger followed Blake inside. It was a deep narrow room. Along one wall were two state-of-the-art computers, each with four 21-inch screens, cluster-mounted.

"Wow," Blake said in awe.

"Double wow," added Roger.

"I see you like the room," Kiddo's voice said excitedly.

"I thought we left you back at the Security Center," Roger said.

"What does it mean to leave a voice behind?"

"Huh?" Blake said.

"Excuse me for being philosophical. It gets lonely around here during the Holidays. Every departmental computer is in hibernate mode. Since I am the Security Center's computer, I never sleep. I never even rest. Besides, I love following things that happen on campus. I can pop up anywhere any time I choose."

"It's nice to know you are watching out for us, Kiddo," Roger said.

"Thank you, but I will leave you to your work, now," Kiddo responded.

Roger sat down and swiveled a full circle in his plush office chair. "I'd better get started."

"So why did you want me here?" Blake asked.

"As I was going through the theory of traveling between inner surfaces of the universe bubble, one strange factor kept popping up. No matter how cleverly I approached the mathematics, this one problem kept getting in the way.

"When I leaped up and said we needed to get into the

Lab, I had just figured out part of it. I don't know why I hadn't seen it sooner."

"This factor involves me, right?" Blake asked.

"It does. And believe me; you are going to have your hands full writing an incredibly important program."

"Okay. Let me have it. What do I need to do?"

"Consider this first, Blake. If travel from place to place on the bubble's inner surface is instantaneous and travel to and from the inner surface is virtually instantaneous, how would someone avoid arriving on the surface of an inhospitable planet—or even worse, on the surface of a star?"

Blake's eyebrows furrowed slightly. "Are you saying that I need to create a program that can, in zero time, detect a safe planet as a destination?"

The keys on Roger's computer clicked away faster than Blake thought possible. Finally, Roger's fingers slowed and then stopped. He pushed away from his desk and exhaled loudly as his shoulders relaxed. "That's a relief," Roger said, still staring at the lower right computer screen. "For a moment there I thought we might have encountered an unsolvable problem."

"What would that problem have been?" Blake inquired.

"I had to figure out how long it would take to travel across the thickness of the universe bubble. If we had to travel from the outside surface it might take hours or days to get to the inner surface and if we happened to be living on the inner surface there might not be enough time at all for your program to find a suitable place to land."

"What did you find out?" Blake asked anxiously.

"Time is measured quite differently when travel is undertaken perpendicular to the bubble. And there is another phenomenon that works in our favor."

"Okay," Blake said, his curiosity mounting. "And what is that?"

"No physical matter, in other words, no galaxies exist right at either surface of the bubble. Therefore, there will always be a little distance—or time—for a vehicle to traverse before getting to the nothing sphere."

Blake sat motionless for a moment as he considered the idea Roger had just presented.

Roger's head bobbed as he began once again to hammer on his computer keyboard. When his hands pulled away, he calmly said. "Light travels at light speed only along the curved *plane* of the bubble." Then he fell silent.

"How fast does light travel perpendicular to the plane?" Blake asked.

"That's just what I was trying to determine, but this much I know—it travels exponentially faster."

"Wow," Blake said.

"And, Blake," Roger continued, "we not only reside on a Goldilocks planet, our galaxy is a Goldilocks galaxy in that it is as near as possible to the inner surface of the universe bubble."

"And that is good?" Blake said hesitantly.

"It is. It means even though your program will need to do some pretty fast calculating it will definitely have *some* time in which to do it. I'm certain writing a program to do that is something you're up to."

"We'll see," Blake said feigning self-doubt.

"I'd also recommend you design your program to find a planet in a similarly located galaxy across the interior void of the bubble. I know that means a very fast determination, but why dillydally around when something incredibly exciting must lie just ahead?"

"Okay," Blake said. "But how quickly must my program find a Goldilocks galaxy, a Goldilocks solar system, and a Goldilocks planet?"

For the next several seconds Roger's fingers attacked his keyboard. "It must make the calculation in no more than 0.008439 seconds."

"Oh," Blake said nonchalantly as he rolled his eyes. "Silly me. I thought it would need to be fast."

Chapter Ten

THE PROJECT BEGINS

"I hope I can make it work within those parameters," Blake said. "But can you eventually determine the precise length of time it will take to travel from the Lab to the bubble's inner surface?"

"Probably, but what I have given you should be close enough. Just allow about half that time to get us to the inner bubble surface and the other half to get us from some other point on the inner surface to a new hospitable planet. In the mean time, I have a lot more theory and mathematics to wade through to get my part done. Even then there are picochips, systems, and parts to design. And then there is assembly and testing."

"Okay, okay. I get the picture. At what point in time do you need my part to be complete?"

"I need your preliminary bio-guidance system designed by the time I finish with the theory, math, and applications," Roger said.

Blake glanced up momentarily at the ceiling. "How long do you think your stuff will take you? Weeks, days, hours?"

"Oh, hours! It must be hours—maybe spread out over a few days."

Blake smirked slightly as his head began to nod. "Actually, I'm sure I can do it, Roger."

"Great. I feel quite good about my part, too."

"Just as a side note, the car can look however we want it to look, can't it?" Blake asked.

"I don't see why not," Roger said. "Does it really matter?"

"I was just thinking about the vehicle in the 1960 movie, *The Time Machine*—the one starring Rod Taylor."

"Yeah, it looked pretty wild."

"Let's make ours look like a common, ordinary, car. Oh, we'll need to include a drive system of some kind," Blake pointed out. "Will it be difficult to find room for one, along with the perpendicular-to-the-universe-bubble mechanisms?"

"I'll make it fit."

"I've been thinking about something else, too," Blake said. "Let's build two vehicles."

"Why?" Roger asked.

"One day we may each want to go exploring on our own."

"That sounds reasonable, but getting just one vehicle completely done by the end of summer quarter will be challenging enough. In the meantime, I need to talk to Kiddo."

"You need something, Roger?" Kiddo responded instantly.

"To what extent may we use the Laboratory and the equipment and materials it contains?"

"Usually, such things are explained at the beginning of each quarter. It is so much fun to see the students who excelled the previous quarter leap out of their chairs as privileges are announced. It was especially fun for me to watch the two of you as you found out an hour or so ago."

"It was exciting for us, too, but what *do* we have access to?"

"Everything. You are the first second-year students in the history of the school to be granted full access to everything!"

"I don't understand," Blake said humbly.

"No two students have ever scored higher in innovation, ingenuity, and creativity and at the same time excelled academically."

"And Roger and I can use any materials or tools contained in the Lab?" Blake asked to make sure he understood.

"Blake, let me put your mind at ease," Kiddo said. "Not only may you use anything in the facility, all you have to do is send me an email listing what you need. I will instantly approve it and send it on to the Procurement Department's computer. It will immediately take itself out of hibernation mode and order whatever you need. Things will be shipped within an hour. They will arrive at your station in the Laboratory the following morning, at the latest."

"Thank you Kiddo," Roger said. "May I assume Blake and I can begin working on our second year project now—a week early—before any other students return after New Year's Day."

"That's right. Your new instructors have already been notified and are aware of your status. You are authorized to begin whenever you choose."

"Thank you, Kiddo," Roger said.

"You are most welcome, but you probably should thank your department head and the Board of Trustees."

"Sure," Blake said. "As if we'll ever meet them."

Kiddo said, "It may come as a surprise, but they are quite anxious to meet you."

"Wow," Roger said.

"Really?" Blake said.

"Really," Kiddo said reassuringly.

Roger said as he rubbed his stomach. "Right now, Blake and I need to have breakfast."

"You mean lunch, don't you?" Kiddo suggested.

Roger glanced at his computer monitor. "You're

right. Blake here slept half the morning away."

"I confess," Blake said. "But then Roger decided that finding out about Lab access was more important than food."

"Thanks for everything, Kiddo," Roger said.

"The same goes for me," Blake added.

"I don't know when we'll be back here to work on the project," Roger said. "It may not be for a few days. Both Blake and I have a lot of theory to verify, research and analysis to complete before beginning to build our second-year project. The next part of the theory I can handle on my computer back at our suite."

"Me too," Blake agreed.

Kiddo said, "Hurry back. There won't be anyone else for me to talk with for another week or so."

"There's always us," Psi and Phi chimed in.

After a hastily thrown-together lunch, Roger said, as he shoved his chair away from the table, "I really need to get back to the project."

"Go ahead and get started," Blake said, motioning his roommate along. "I'll take care of cleaning up."

"Hey, what about us?" Psi said.

"Yeah. You said you would need our help," Phi added. "I remember, Roger."

"Your memory is correct. Actually, when I said it, I wasn't sure just how you two were going to fit in, but I have a hunch Blake knows what we need you two to do."

Blake was caught off guard but did some fast thinking.

"Okay," Blake began after Roger left the room. "In a week and a half, winter quarter will begin. By the first day of class each pair of second-year students must turn in an outline of their sophomore project. What we need you two to do is develop a decoy project."

"Ah," Psi said suspiciously. "You want us to lie and to deceive."

Blake said, "No, no way. You two must come up with and develop a legitimate, worthwhile project worthy of the top two second-year students at IPI. Obviously it will need to be incorporated into a vehicle. Not the one Roger and I will be working on, but the second car we'll be leaving behind in the lab."

"Oh," Phi said solemnly. "You really do need some help. So, what's wrong with your darting-across-the-universe project?"

"Though the theory seems solid, we have yet to determine if we can actually build a vehicle that will *dart across the universe*, as you put it," Blake said. "It might consume all of our time just to find out for sure. By then, even if it works, it may be too late to complete the car, hence, the need for a simpler backup project. So, will you handle the second project?"

Psi said confidently, "We will not let you down."

"Good. Now I need to finish the dishes."

Before Blake went to his room he peeked in on Roger, who was typing furiously at the keyboard, his head bobbing slightly as he seemed to be agreeing with ideas as they flowed through his fingers.

Blake turned to his own room and computer. He pulled up the most advanced program he had created while yet in high school—the one he had used to design the biochips that had earned him the scholarship to IPI.

When the program was fully installed and functioning, Blake set to work adapting and expanding it into the most sophisticated biochip he had ever dreamed of creating. As his fingers flew across the keys ideas flooded into his mind—most of which he had never entertained before.

Finally, Blake paused to shake out his hands. He was surprised to see it was dark outside. A glance at the clock in the bottom corner of his computer monitor informed him he had worked for five uninterrupted hours.

He got up and arched his back as he stretched his arms high overhead. He left his room and glanced into Roger's.

Roger was lying at an angle on his bed. His wrists were crossed over his forehead and his right foot was flat on the floor. As Blake turned toward the living room, Roger stirred. "How did your session go?" he called out.

Blake turned back. "It was amazing. I felt—how should I put it?—inspired. I mean I had ideas and concepts surging into my mind. Many of them were entirely new to me and, quite frankly, challenged my comprehension."

"I had a similar experience," Roger said. "Uncanny."

"Are you ready for dinner?"

"Sure, but I don't feel like cooking. Let's go get a burger or something," Roger said.

"Grab your coat."

Blake and Roger slipped their super smart phones into their pockets and soon climbed into Roger's car. "Where shall we eat?" Roger asked.

"Let's go to Bumpkin Billy's Burger Barn," Blake suggested. "It's always fun and diverting."

Blake and Roger approached the counter, which was made to look like a long stack of baled hay. A cute girl, dressed like Daisy Mae, appearing as if just stepping out of a Li'l Abner comic strip, took their orders, after which the boys seated themselves near the back.

Soon thereafter, Bumpkin Billy himself arrived with a tray filled with food and drinks. As usual, he tripped and stumbled as he approached. The tray headed straight for them. However, each item was a prop and fastened securely to the tray. For some reason, the gag never seemed to get too old.

Right behind Bumpkin Billy, another Daisy Mae look-alike arrived at their booth. "Here is your order, gentlemen."

Roger reached for the tray and spread the food onto the table. "So Psi and Phi, have you come up with a good cover-up project?"

Psi announced proudly, "Yes we have, and we don't have to lie about it."

"Lie?" Roger asked.

"Blake can explain later," Psi said, "Now, Blake, I began by digging through all of your old high school notes, files, and journals—the ones archived with Carbonite-Vault. I selected a most incredible project."

"Great," Blake said. "Explain it to us while we eat."

"Psi, go ahead. You found the idea," Phi said.

"As the two of you know, one challenge with car guidance has been unmanned steering."

"They've already solved that problem," Roger said.

"Hey. I remember back when I had that idea," Blake inserted. "It was about the same time industry came up with a solution, but Roger's right. That problem has been solved."

"Sure," Psi said, "for major highways and city streets. But there are thousands and thousands of miles of minor highways, rural roads, and unpaved recreational trails."

"Not to mention people's driveways littered with children's toys or greasy garage floors cluttered with tools and the like," Phi added.

"And you two have figured out how to create a steering system that works anywhere and under all conditions—without human involvement?" Roger asked.

"Indeed, we have," Phi said proudly.

Psi asked, "Do you think it is a good enough project for two humble geniuses?"

Blake glanced at Roger. They smiled at each other

and said almost simultaneously, "We're flattered."

"You guys are pompous! That's what you are." Psi declared boldly.

Phi added, "We were referring to ourselves."

"Okay, okay" Roger said, "But can you really make it work? If you can, yes, it's definitely good enough."

"Of course one or both of you will have to do the hands-on parts, but we'll generate detailed schematics, drawings, and instructions," Psi stated.

Blake said, "As fast as things came together for me this afternoon, I'll get to it within the next few days. I assume your solution depends on biochips, is that right, Psi?"

"Precisely," Phi said. "The only way to steer through absolutely any course on any road is by means of some kind of intelligence and artificial intelligence is good enough, no offence intended."

Blake said, "Sounds like a challenge, though."

Roger added, "I'll take care of the mechanical parts. Let me know when you need them."

After dinner, Blake and Roger returned to the dormitory tower and replanted themselves in front of their computers.

Chapter Eleven

THE PROJECT TAKES ON NEW PURPOSE

Blake stopped working on his biochip design long enough to rub his eyes and take a few slow breaths.

Roger appeared at his door yawning. "I'm ready to call it a day," he said. "How about you?"

"My brain is definitely calling for a rest."

Roger said, "Blake, as long as we're taking a break, I want to bounce something off you. We've been so busy the past few days that I haven't found an opportunity until now"

Blake turned in his chair and Roger sat on the edge of Blake's bed.

"What's on your mind, Roger?"

"Christmas Day, while I waited for my parents to return to their apartment, I went shopping. That's when I bumped into the old friend of mine I mentioned a couple days ago. His mother was killed during a robbery at the small store his family runs in my old neighborhood."

"I'm sorry to hear that, Roger."

"I was too, but what also concerned me was that after his mother was murdered, his father turned even more frequently to the bottle. That left my friend running the store and he's my age."

"Wow," Blake said as he got up and headed for the kitchen. "Keep talking. I'm listening."

Roger spoke a little louder. "A week or so ago his dad happened to meet some Mormons who are trying to help him. It seems odd to me that members of such a strange church would care about a total stranger."

Blake returned with two cans of soda pop. He handed one to Roger. "It doesn't surprise me. It's probably typical of most churches."

Roger pulled the tab on the top of his can and took a drink. "What amazed me most though was he said his father has committed to getting off the bottle. And he said it wouldn't surprise him if his dad would reach out to my parents and help them with their problems."

"That would be great," Blake said smiling.

"I'd like to know one thing though, Blake. Will they help, or are they just looking for another convert?"

"I'm sure they're serious about trying to help."

Roger's shoulders seem to relax. "I hope they are and

I hope they succeed."

Blake said, "My dad's problems may not be that bad, but I wish someone would help him. He always seems ready to argue with me about a mission. I can't see what the rush is all about. I won't turn eighteen for sixteen months. Oh, that's not the real issue. I really want to complete my studies first. But that will take over three years. Dad thinks that that's too long to wait."

"I can see his point of view, especially if he is convinced your church is God's church," Roger said and then paused. "Is it?"

Blake was caught off guard. He shook his head slightly as he glanced down at the floor. "I'm not sure," Blake said quietly.

"Good grief, Blake. I always figured you were just being stubborn, but you really don't want to go on that mission."

"Not you too, Roger. It was a very frustrating discussion with my dad on this same subject that made me decide to head back to school a week and a half early."

"I can tell I've hit a nerve, Blake," Roger said. "I'm sorry. Would you mind talking about something else then, even if it is religion-related?"

"Sure, Roger," Blake said, relieved at a change of subject.

"Once we had this crazy conversation about God. Psi quoted something out of one of your Mormon books. I didn't pay much attention to what he said at the time let alone where he found it."

Blake asked, "What was it about?"

"It had something to do with God or Christ creating other planets just like the one we live on."

Blake shrugged. "Well, Psi, where is it?"

Instantly, Psi said, "*Pearl of Great Price*, Book of Moses, chapter 1, verse 33. It says '...worlds without number have I created....'"

"That's far enough," Roger said interrupting. "Does this mean that these worlds are all populated with people just like you and me?" Roger asked.

Blake nodded reluctantly as he realized that agreeing was, in a way, bearing his testimony.

"Do you realize what that means, Blake?"

Blake wasn't sure where Roger was going with this question, so he was evasive. "What does it mean to you?"

"It means that if the vehicle we're going to build performs the way we plan and if God is as your church teaches, we may very well arrive on one of those worlds He created. I find it not only a bit scary, but I think He just might view us as trespassers. I would not want His wrath to crash down on us."

Blake sat silently for a long time.

"Isn't that what that scripture implies?" Roger asked.

"What?" Blake responded, "that God's wrath may crush us?"

"No, not that," Roger replied, "the part about all those worlds. Do you think we might find and land on one of them?"

"I suppose it's possible," Blake responded hesitantly.

"Don't you know? It's your church and your scriptures and your doctrine. How come you don't know, Blake? I would have thought you had it all figured out since it was your idea in the first place, to visit a planet clear across the universe."

"It never occurred to me to travel across the universe, let alone to visit another planet," Blake declared defensively. "I simply had this idea about perpendicular-to-the-universe travel."

Roger got up, shaking his head. "But why didn't it cross your mind where your idea might lead?"

Blake shrugged. "How should I know? Probably because my mind just happened to wander on Christmas Eve. Besides, it never occurred to me that it might really be possible to go skipping around the universe, Roger. I had no idea the concept had any merit until you told me it was plausible."

"You're right. I'm sorry, Blake."

"That's okay."

As Roger got up to leave the room, he said, "I'm calling it a day. I'll see you in the morning."

Blake remained seated at his desk, staring at where Roger had been sitting and thinking about what Roger had concluded about this fantastic doctrine of the Church. Blake suddenly realized he had taken many religious teachings for granted for all too long.

After several minutes Blake slid off his chair, turned

around, and with his forearms resting on his desk, he knelt in prayer.

It snowed heavily for the next several days. But early Sunday morning—the day before classes were to resume, the sun shone so brightly that when Blake awoke his first thought was that he must have slept in—until noon.

Roger was in the kitchen. Blake heard the faint clinking of Lucky Charms, each fighting to be first into the bowl.

Blake entered the kitchen, still in his pajamas, rubbing his eyes. "Good morning, Roger."

"It's about time. I would have thought you would be up and going by now."

"Now that I think about it, my alarm hasn't gone off yet."

Just then there were the soft sounds of several harp strings followed by Psi saying, "Blake, you're up early for a change, it is a Sunday after all. What are your plans for the day?"

"I was just about to see what Roger had in mind."

"I'm going to spend my day in the Lab. I've worked through all the math and theory behind traveling across the perpendicular-to-the-universe bubble and I'm going to begin laying out the electronics and building the parts. Oh, by the way, I'm tired of referring to it as the *perpendicular-to-the-universe-bubble device,* so from now on, to me at least, it's the PTB-drive mechanism."

"That sounds cool enough. I guess I'm ready for the Lab too," Blake said.

"So am I," Psi said.

"I am too," Phi added.

Blake said, "I'll jump in the shower and be back in a few minutes."

The Laboratory Building was no longer totally silent. Here and there professors, instructors, and upper-class students traversed the halls, even though it was a Sunday.

Blake was shocked when one of them cheerfully said, "Oh, you are Blake and Roger, right?"

"Yes," Roger responded. "And you are James Noddington—but you don't go by Jim."

"That's correct. I am so glad I bumped into the two of you this morning. Did you know I have been assigned to be your second-year project advisor?"

"No," Blake said.

"That's exciting," Roger responded. Turning to his roommate, he continued, "James is among the top fifth-year students here at the Institute."

"I know," Blake said. "I'm excited too."

"Thank you," James said. "You know, we have something in common. My fifth-year and your second-year projects must be incredible."

Roger asked, "Is yours?"

"Of course, but I'm keeping the details a secret. In fact, I've told my faculty advisor very little about it."

Blake looked at Roger who returned a big smile.

"So, what is *your* project?" James asked.

"Well," Blake began slowly. "We feel much the same as you do. We hope to keep the details a secret for as long as we can."

James said, "But the outline and scope of your project must be in my hands by 10:00 tomorrow morning."

"It will be," Blake said as he and Roger walked away grinning.

The snow drifts and piles along the roads melted slowly as winter gave way to the first day of spring.

The previous two and a half months seemed to pass in a matter of a few weeks. Blake and Roger had spent a seemingly endless string of half-days in class and half-days, all evenings, and weekends in the Lab.

The chassis, interior, and bodywork of both cars were finished, including painting. They appeared identical.

Psi and Phi had completed the secondary project with ease weeks ago. It was now successfully installed into the second car, but the omni-directional steering system was yet to be tested.

Roger's PTB-drive mechanism had recently been installed in the first car, but it was also untested.

Blake's part was finished as well, but not to his satisfaction. This was causing him restless nights filled with fitful sleep.

It was noon the first Friday in April. The snow was

gone. Warm sunny days were becoming the norm.

Roger and Blake left the testing center. Their last final was over. The campus roads were busy as most students were on their way—to anywhere—as long as it was away from school. The next week and a half was the annual spring break and the majority of the student body would soon be playing volleyball on some Florida beach or surfing just off the southern California coast.

Blake unlocked their suite door, and he and his roommate entered. "I'm not sure why, but I don't feel entirely comfortable with the biochips I've been working on the past few months."

"What seems to be the problem?" Roger inquired.

Blake said, "Perhaps it's just a wrinkle in my self-confidence, but it is absolutely imperative that these chips function 100% as designed. If I fail to get everything right, I could get both of us killed."

"If either of us gets anything seriously wrong, we each might die," Roger said matter-of-factly.

Blake tossed his sweater on the sofa. He reached into his shirt pocket. It was empty. His eyes fastened onto Roger's eyes. "I just unlocked the door."

"So what? I know I didn't do it," Roger said.

"I used my key!" Blake said emphatically as he checked his shirt pocket again. He reached for his sweater and searched its pockets. He felt all four of the pants' pockets. "Psi's missing."

Roger checked his pockets.

"What's going on here?" Blake insisted.

"I can scarcely believe it," Roger said chuckling.

"You can scarcely believe what? Is Phi missing as well?" Blake demanded.

Roger nodded as a smile crept across his face. Then he began to bob his head. "There is only one plausible explanation as to why they are missing. And the thought is intriguing."

"What's that?"

"You know how they've been exhibiting abilities and personalities beyond what you designed into them?"

"Yeah," Blake said. "It's been going on for months."

"Wouldn't it be amazing if they have developed the ability to implant ideas into our minds. Maybe they can even remove them."

Blake demanded, "Are you suggesting they prevented us from placing them into our pockets?"

Roger nodded. "Do you have a better explanation?"

Blake paused for a moment and then he began to smile too. "I'll bet you're right. Let's go back and get those two rascals."

Roger shook his head. "Why not wait until this evening?"

"Why wait?" Blake asked.

"Let's give them enough time to finish whatever it is they are up to."

"Yeah," Blake agreed slyly.

Chapter Twelve

TO THE LAB AND BEYOND

The front door to the Laboratory Building opened slowly and quietly. It was as if Blake and Roger were expected.

"Hi, Kiddo," Blake whispered. "Do you know anything about two renegade pocket computers?"

"Oh, I've been keeping an eye on them and listening to what they have been saying. It was obvious they were up to something neither of you knew about," Kiddo said, her decibel level adjusted low.

Roger asked, "They have no idea we're creeping up on them?"

Kiddo said, "I think they have been so busy they haven't even given a thought to the possibility *I* might eavesdrop. Besides, if they knew I was listening in it might have spoiled their fun."

"So they are having fun, are they?" Blake said.

"Oh, yes indeed. I've never seen bio-computers like these two."

"Well, Roger, shall we go see what they have been up to?" Blake asked.

Roger nodded.

Blake and Roger crept around the last corner of the corridor leading to the laboratory space specifically assigned to them. The upper half of the hallway was made of glass so students could pause and watch what other students were working on.

The lights inside the lab were out. The hall lights illuminated the lab just enough for Blake and Roger to conclude that nothing observable was going on inside.

"I don't understand," Blake said. "From what Kiddo said, I was expecting—something—I don't know what."

Roger shrugged. "I don't get it either."

"Let's check things out," Blake said as he pushed the Lab door open. The entire room was suddenly brightly illuminated.

"Surprise, Blake!" Psi and Phi called out, their voices amplified through the overhead speakers, which usually played music.

"Okay," Blake said hesitantly. "I'm surprised, I guess. What am I surprised about?"

"Yeah," Roger added. "So what's the surprise?"

"Blake, come over to your workbench," Psi said. "You'll see."

As Blake approached his work area, his computer's monitor flashed on. Blake found his eyes glued to the screen. The words on it read as follows:

> Happy 17th Birthday, Blake! Though this wish is several days early, my gift to you is what I have done to your biochip design. I am quite sure you will no longer worry about it not working.
> Psi

"What have you done?!" Blake cried out.

"I knew you were worried about whether your biochip design would actually prevent your car from landing somewhere inhospitable. So, I examined each of your chips."

"And…?" Blake said.

"I found several mistakes…," Psi began.

Phi interrupted. "They weren't really mistakes, Blake. Psi simply found better, safer, and faster ways of getting the same things done."

"Phi's right. The way you had things there were weaknesses. So, I fixed them. And I had new biochips made and installed using the Lab's mobile robots."

Roger shook his head as he planted his fists on his hips. "What about my designs, Phi? I suppose you found

119

flaws in them as well?"

Phi responded meekly, "Actually I did, but don't feel bad, Roger. Making mistakes happens to be a very common human behavior."

Blake and Roger stared at one another.

"What do you say we disassemble these two characters, Roger? I think they've gotten too big for their britches."

"We don't wear britches or pants or trousers or anything like that," Psi declared merrily.

Blake picked Psi up and spoke to him as if he was a microphone. "You know what I mean."

"Yes, I do," Psi said. "But stop and think about what we have accomplished, okay?"

"Oh," Blake said. "You are proud to have outdone us, right?"

"Perhaps," Psi said, "But there's more to it than that."

Roger said, "You want to graduate with honors in our places. Is that it?"

"Stop kidding around," Psi said. "What we have done is finish your project."

"Psi is right," Phi said. "All of the other second-year students have three months now to work out the bugs and get their project vehicles operating smoothly."

"And," Psi added, "Since yours is done, Phi and I took the liberty to notify the Evaluation and Advancement Board's computer that your project is complete. They have scheduled your project presentation and defense for this coming Monday morning: 10:00 a.m. to be exact."

"How could you take that upon yourselves?!" Blake demanded.

"Why not? The project is done, isn't it?" Phi asked.

"Sure," Blake answered, "but I would have thought that the faculty, who serve on the Board, would have gone on spring break too."

"Most of them had or were about to," Psi said, "but once it was known that you two had completed your project so early, enough faculty members to constitute a quorum decided to begin their holiday a few days late."

Roger said, "But what if something goes wrong and our project doesn't work?"

"Nothing is going to go wrong," Psi stated emphatically.

"And Psi and I are probably as excited as you are to see what lies on the other side of the universe," Phi pointed out.

"Are you serious?" Blake asked skeptically.

"I think they are," Roger said. "And why shouldn't they be? Aren't you?"

Blake stood still for a moment, his head slowly shaking. Finally he plopped down in the chair in front of his Lab computer. He pressed a key and stared silently as screen after screen appeared, each pausing just long enough for Blake to see how Psi had altered and improved the biochip circuitry.

He finally looked up, after the last screen faded away, and glanced to the side. Roger too had been reviewing the displays on his computer monitor. He rubbed his forehead as his head gradually swayed side to side.

"Hello in there, Blake and Roger. It means we can begin exploring the universe today. And I mean right now. Just climb into the car and let's go," Phi suggested.

Blake said, "But we haven't had dinner yet."

"Good try," Psi said. "I'll bet there will be food on the very first planet we visit. Trust me."

"Trust you?" Blake said.

"Well, the least you can do is to trust your new and improved biochips," Psi said. "I certainly do."

"Me too," Phi said. "Quit stalling. Let's go!"

Roger climbed behind the steering wheel and Blake slid into the passenger's seat. Once they were comfortably situated with their seat belts and shoulder straps securely fastened, the doors lowered into place.

Phi was inserted into a slot just left of center on the dash board and Psi was slipped into a slot to the right.

"Is everyone ready?" Roger asked.

"I am," Psi and Phi responded in unison.

Psi said, "I'm not sure about Blake. His heart is racing and his body temperature is rising."

"Okay, Phi," Roger said. "Drive us out into the countryside while Blake calms down."

"Sure," Phi responded.

Psi added, "Good idea. Some pleasant scenery might calm his nerves."

"I sure hope so," Blake said. "I don't want to hold up

this trans-universal adventure."

Phi steered the car toward the outskirts of town.

"Blake," Phi said. "As you have probably concluded, this vehicle will not leap across the universe until its occupants' vital signs are within certain parameters. It can now sense human anxiety and is programmed not to add to it."

Psi added, "That is one of the refinements I made. Humans tend to see themselves as brave and courageous when they anticipate the distant future. But the present is something else altogether."

"All right," Blake said, deliberately slowing his breathing and relaxing his body.

Suddenly the screen in front of Blake lit up and there were his vital signs.

"Good," Psi said. "Breathe more slowly. I promise you that this vehicle will function exactly as you and Roger designed it. There is nothing to be afraid of."

Blake rolled his eyes. "Duh. The unknown has always been feared by mankind."

"Of course, you're right, Blake," Psi confessed. "But I suggest this is different. What is about to happen may involve things unknown, but you may rest assured, all will be well."

"How can you be so sure, Psi?" Roger asked.

"You two have followed all the rules, haven't you? Isn't it a little bit like following those commandments Blake talks about—the ones found in Exodus?"

Roger snickered. "Don't tell me you're a Mormon,

too, Psi?"

"Oh, that. You're surprised to learn I know what the Bible says?"

"Yeah," Roger responded. "Totally."

"Blake installed the *Gospel Library* App in me when he finished designing my biochips." Then Psi's voice dropped to a whisper. "Blake doesn't refer to that library very often, but I do, and I keep the App up to date. Actually, I am way ahead of him when it comes to religious knowledge."

"And you are convinced we will have a safe trip?" Roger asked calmly.

"Absolutely. Both of you have exhibited incredible faith and amazing effort. Faith and works are essential to the achievement of all worthwhile undertakings."

"I suppose so," Roger said.

"Blake, check out the monitor," Phi said. "See, your vital signs are almost normal. I'll park the car just beyond those trees."

Blake focused on the screen and continued willing himself to be at peace. The moment the last of his vital signs registered normal, the vehicle began to hum.

A vertical column of circles appeared on Roger's monitor. The first one was followed by the word, CLEARANCE. The second was followed by the word, JUXTAPOSE. A third was followed by STATUS, a fourth by the word RETURN, and a fifth by ABORT.

Roger said, "What's the ABORT button all about?"

Psi answered, "You will never have to push that one,

Roger. Either Phi or I will activate it instantaneously if the need arises. It's there just so you will know what is happening in the event that it begins flashing."

"Oh well" Roger said calmly. "I guess it's about time to press CLEARANCE. What exactly does it mean, Psi?"

"The computers on board will check all systems to make sure they are working properly, and Blake's biochips will instantly scan for a suitable destination point. When the CLEARANCE button turns green press the JUXTAPOSE button," Psi instructed.

"And get ready for the most incredible experience of your life," Phi added. "Unfortunately the trip will last only a few milliseconds, at most. Actually, it is not the trip that counts. It's the destination and what happens there."

While Roger inhaled deeply, Psi asked, "What do you two anticipate, anyway?"

Roger remained quiet.

Blake said, "If this whole operation works, I expect to soon be wondering if we have left earth at all."

"Very perceptive," Psi said. "Phi and I have discussed this at length and after examining all your Mormon doctrine, we came to the same conclusion."

"Roger, the CLEARANCE button is green. We aren't going anywhere until you press the second button," Phi said.

"I know that adding this screen is one of the things you and Psi did this afternoon. It is wonderful. But, why does this one say JUXTAPOSE?"

Psi answered. "We are not really traveling much at all, are we? We are simply moving sideways relative to the plane of the universal bubble. Phi and I couldn't think of a better word to describe moving to the side."

Blake watched as Roger's hand slowly moved toward the screen.

The moment he touched it Blake saw a slight flash of light and a brief chill shot through his body. His eyes were shut, he thought, but were they really? He concluded they were open, but for a split second, there was nothing to see—for that instant, time ceased to exist.

Then Blake's awareness shifted to the very abstract. *If an instant was divided into an infinite number of divisions how long would it take to traverse them all— taking them one at a time?*

Blake had heard this concept discussed by his classmates on numerous occasions. It was an intellectually entertaining way to spend an evening.

Inevitably, the only conclusion was that it would take an infinite amount to time to pass by an infinite number of time increments regardless of how long or short the time intervals being considered.

And then Blake had his sight again. He could scarcely believe his eyes. "Oh, my!" he exclaimed. "I never really imagined...."

Chapter Thirteen

ARE WE THERE YET?

Blake paused only a moment to dig his knuckles into his eyes, his brain attempting to believe that the pastoral landscape he beheld was anything other than a masterpiece by one of the greatest painters of all time and was being projected onto the inner surface of the windshield.

He glanced over at Roger, whose hand was just leaving the JUXTAPOSE button. The word ABORT was no longer next to its button, but had been replaced by the word BIO-DRIVE. Roger pressed this button next.

The vehicle moved forward along the right side of a

country road.

"Did this thing work?" Roger asked as he gazed out the his window. "I'd swear we are cruising through the rolling hills of Kentucky."

"Yeah," Blake said pointing. "Just around that bend, I bet we see a split-rail fence surrounding a verdant pasture of grazing stallions."

"Of course, it worked," Psi said.

"How else can you explain that at one moment it was dark outside and now it is broad daylight? About noon, I'd say," Phi added.

"Okay," Roger responded a little reluctantly.

Just before they reached the bend, a vehicle not noticeably different from the one they were in, came placidly around the curve toward them and passed on their left. Its passengers waved cordially.

"This is not what *I* anticipated," Roger stated. "But look at the screen. It says, DESTINATION ACHIEVED: PLANET EARTH-126,871. Why the number?"

"I could guess," Blake said.

"You needn't guess, Blake," Psi began. "A few months ago when I was quoting from the Book of Moses, Roger interrupted me before I finished. Verse 35 is quite interesting in regards to these numberless worlds. It says, *For behold, there are many worlds that have passed away by the word of my power. And there are many that now stand, and innumerable are they unto man; but all things are numbered unto me, for they are mine and I know them.*"

Roger said. "That's what I would have guessed. God's *worlds without number* are numbered to Him."

Blake suddenly called out. "Look! There *is* a split-rail fence! And—a pasture full of the most beautiful horses I have ever seen! And I've seen lots. My uncle raises horses."

The vehicle slowed and pulled off the road at a point where the best view of the horses could be seen. Blake and Roger stared in wonder as the horses approached.

"Psi, could the locator component of the guidance computer be wrong? Could this still be planet earth—the one Roger and I grew up on?"

"No, Blake. We have traveled many, many light years as the crow flies—I mean as perpendicular-to-the-bubble light shines. We are no longer on the Earth upon which you grew up. Obviously *The Pearl of Great Price* has it right," Psi explained.

"Look over there," Phi said. "Look out Blake's window."

Blake and Roger turned away from the horses that they had been admiring.

"Oh, my," Blake said. "Now I understand what has happened. This vehicle induces dreams."

"Let's check it out, Blake," Roger said.

The vehicle's onboard computer picked up on the boys' conversation and the doors lifted and folded back. Blake and Roger climbed out, hurried across the road, and walked onto grass as soft as crushed velvet.

Roger spoke first. "Hello," he called out.

Blake quickly responded, "They won't be able to understand you. Surely then must speak a different language here."

"Huh?" Roger muttered.

Two of the most beautiful young women Blake had ever seen, or could even imagine, rose gracefully from a blanket spread evenly over the grassy carpet.

"Hello," the fair-skinned, blond girl said.

"You...a...speak...English?" Blake muttered.

"No," the girl said. "Those devices you carry in your shirt pockets are transferring our thoughts to you and yours to us in the form of spoken language."

Blake stared skeptically at his shirt pocket. He whispered, "Can you do that?"

Psi said nothing but Blake clearly heard in his mind. *"You'd be surprised what Phi and I can do."*

Blake recalled the experience he and Roger had had just that afternoon when they had arrived at their dormitory suite without realizing they had left Psi and Phi behind at the laboratory. *"Maybe I wouldn't be surprised at all,"* Blake thought back.

The brunette said, "Come share the picnic we have prepared for you."

"You fixed lunch for us?" Roger asked.

"Yes," the blond said. "Early this morning, we felt prompted to prepare a picnic for four, and to set it out here. We have been waiting for you."

"And you brought food?" Blake asked.

130

"It wouldn't be much of a picnic without it," the brunette said. "

Blake and Roger shrugged at each other.

"By the way, my name is Alee-aLauna," the blond girl said. "This is my sister, Shay-Leah."

The boys introduced themselves.

"Please make yourselves comfortable," Alee-aLauna said as her companion removed a small red and white checkered cloth from a wicker basket. Beneath it were several pieces of fried chicken, salad, rolls, and what looked like some sort of dessert.

While Blake and Roger filled their plates, Shay-Leah said, "Alee-aLauna was named after the wife of one of our early prophets. His name was Sordilee. I was named after her sister."

Alee-aLauna added, "The name Shay-Leah is as close as our language gets to the name Sariah. Perhaps you have heard of her."

For a moment, Blake was speechless. He squinted his eyes just a little as he tipped his head to one side. "You mean as in the *Book of Mormon*?"

"Sure," Shay-Leah said. "We have copies of all your scriptures. And we read and study them."

Blake shook his head as if to clear it of cobwebs. "I don't get it."

"What is there not to get?" Alee-aLauna asked. "Just because you knew nothing about us, doesn't preclude us knowing something about you. Certainly you can relate this to the time Christ told the Nephites that the Jews knew nothing about them."

Roger looked to Blake as if for some kind of explanation—or clarification.

Blake squinted his eyes and furrowed his brows. "Roger, remember yesterday when you suggested we might find ourselves on one of the countless worlds God has created? Well, we must be on one."

Roger smiled in a strange way. "I had already reached that conclusion." Then, raising his eyebrows he peered into Blake's eyes. "So, it's all true."

"What is?" Blake asked.

Roger continued. "Joseph Smith was a prophet, your church is true, God is real, instantaneous travel across the universe is possible, there are worlds without number, this is another of them, and...."

"If you think that that is tough to grasp," Psi said interrupting, "just listen to what verse 34 says. *And the first man of all men have I called Adam, which is many.*"

Roger's eyes rolled upward, his head shaking slowly.

"That's right," Alee-aLauna said. "Each planet has its own Adam and Eve. Each planet had its own fall and need for a Redeemer. The person you know as Christ, the one who lived and was crucified on your planet, is also the Savior of all the repentant on my planet and on *worlds without number*, as your Book of Moses states. This same Christ frequently visits our temples."

"You have seen Christ?" Blake asked excitedly.

"No, silly," Alee-aLauna said as she offered Blake more fried chicken. "I am only seventeen. One must be eighteen to receive a temple recommend. And with a recommend, worthy members do vicarious work for those who have died without hearing about or accepting the Gospel. Besides, Christ visits our temples to communicate personally with the leaders of His church."

Shay-Leah grinned and giggled as she said, "Alee-aLauna is *not* one of our Church's leaders."

Roger wiped his mouth with a napkin.

"Is there anything else I can get you, Roger?" Alee-aLauna asked. "If you are ready for dessert, try these."

Roger accepted a ball of some kind of pastry which had been rolled in powdered sugar. "Thank you," he said.

"What amazes me," Blake began. "is that we've built a vehicle to take us across the universe and here we are and everything I see seems just like home. And yet this is not home."

"If you mean as on Earth-121,673, no, you are definitely not at home," Shay-Leah said.

Blake sat up straight and pulled back slightly. "Earth-121,673?"

"Oh, I'm sorry," Shay-Leah said. "You didn't realize your planet had a number, did you?"

"No, but our vehicle's dashboard screen noted something about *Planet Earth* followed by some numbers."

"That was most likely the number of our planet," Shay-Leah said.

Psi inserted, "The screen said, DESTINATION

ACHIEVED: PLANET EARTH-126,871."

Alee-aLauna commented pleasantly, "This planet is Earth-126,871. It seems ours was created after yours."

Roger rubbed his stomach and reached for more dessert.

Lunch was over and the sun began its trek toward the horizon.

Blake leaned back against an elm tree. It was like the ones back home, only it seemed to be perfectly shaped and all of the leaves were the same deep shade of green. Here and there clumps of colorful flowers adorned the landscape as far as the eye could see.

Blake said, "The beauty of your world reminds me of what the Garden of Eden must have been like."

"Oh," Alee-aLauna exclaimed. "The Garden of Eden is even more beautiful than this."

"How would you know that?" Blake asked.

"We still have ours."

Blake exclaimed, "Are you serious?"

Alee-aLauna nodded reassuringly. "Would you like to see it?"

Blake looked inquiringly at Roger, who said, "We really must get back to our planet. We were only taking our vehicle on a test run and will be missed if we don't return this evening."

Shay-Leah smiled, "It doesn't seem to me that the principles of time which made it possible for you to visit us are known on your planet, but they are well known to

134

the people on our planet. Alee-aLauna and I studied them in middle school."

"You did?" Blake responded, totally amazed.

Shay-Leah nodded. "For centuries, our scientists have known how to travel across the Spherical Void, as we call it. One trip took them to your planet and they returned with your scriptures. That's when we first knew the number assigned to your planet."

Roger interrupted. "So, how does time work—when a person travels perpendicular to the universe bubble?"

Alee-aLauna said. "As for time differences between our planets, since you arrived by traveling across no space, which took no time, you are still in a state of *no-time*."

"I don't understand," Roger began. "If Blake and I return to our planet in a week, we will arrive at the moment we left. Is that what you are saying?"

"Yes," Alee-aLauna said.

"And if we came back to visit you in a week, we'd arrive at the moment we left?"

"No," Shay-Leah said. "Our time would go forward just like yours would."

Roger ran his fingers through his hair while slowly shaking his head. "I don't get it."

"Roger," Alee-aLauna said. "You don't need to understand it completely. Just enjoy it. You wouldn't want it to be any more complicated than how I just explained it, would you?"

"No, no, at least not for the moment. Actually, I kind

of like the idea," Roger said, checking with Blake.

"I like it too," Blake said. "Nonetheless, I agree with Roger. We shouldn't stay too long—not the first time."

Roger added excitedly, "I'd really like to see this Garden of Eden, though."

"Me too," Blake said.

"Of course, it's up to you," Shay-Leah said. "But you certainly don't have to rush back the moment lunch is over, do you?"

Blake shook his head.

"I'll tell you what," Alee-aLauna said. "Why don't you consider this: stay the night, visit the Garden with us in the morning, spend the day, remain for dinner, and then go home tomorrow evening?"

"That sounds like a great compromise," Shay-Leah said. "Then once you've returned to your planet you can begin preparing to visit us again."

"Besides," Alee-aLauna said. "Shay-Leah and I are still in school. We wouldn't be around to entertain you anyway."

Blake glanced at his roommate. "What do you think?"

"I'm game."

"Is it all settled?" Shay-Leah asked. Then seeing a little hesitation in the expression on Roger's face, she asked, "What is it, Roger?"

"It may be settled, but I'm still stuck back on this time thing. Let's see if I have it right. We, Blake and I, could spend a whole day here and still return to our planet at the very moment we left?"

136

"*Almost* the very moment—a tiny amount of time will have passed," Alee-aLauna said.

"This is where it get's tricky for me," Roger said. "So if we were to leave tomorrow, at say 7:00 p.m., we would arrive home at about 8:00 p.m. our earth time today, because that is when we left?"

"Right," Alee-aLauna said. "But let me save you some time and brain-strain. You could not return here until at least 7:00 p.m. your time, the following day. Otherwise, you might meet yourselves here and that paradox is not possible."

"Let's go for it," Blake said. "This should be fun. But where will we stay the night?"

"You are staying with our Aunt La-Deeda," Alee-aLauna said. "She is recently widowed and has twin sons who are serving missions. She would be happy for the company of two young men to sort of fill the void left by her boys' absence."

"Great," Roger said. "Perhaps there are some things around her house we can do for her to repay her for her hospitality."

Chapter Fourteen

MEETING THE FAMILY

"Do you live far from here?" Roger asked after the picnic was over and the basket repacked with the food that had not been eaten.

"No," Alee-aLauna said. "We live across the road; just beyond the fenced-in horses you were watching earlier."

"They are beautiful animals," Blake said. "My Uncle George has horses on his ranch just outside Heber, Utah. I used to love it when our family visited him. Even though I always ended up saddle sore, it was worth the discomfort."

"How about you, Roger?" Alee-aLauna asked.

"The only live horses I've ever seen were either ridden by police officers or were part of some float, being pulled down Central Park West."

"I take it that that's a no; you have never ridden a horse."

Roger shook his head. "But I wouldn't mind trying it if someone will show me how."

Alee-aLauna exchanged glances with her sister. "One of us will help you. Meanwhile, Shay-Leah and I will pack another picnic lunch for tomorrow, we'll saddle up some horses, and then we'll take a leisurely ride to the Garden."

"You do understand," Shay-Leah said, "that we can not enter the Garden."

"Of course not," Blake said.

Roger seemed a bit disappointed. "I don't know much about religion, but I sure would like to walk through a Garden of Eden."

"I'm sorry, Roger. It just can't be done," Shay-Leah said.

"Oh well. I was just telling you how I feel."

Blake and Roger walked with their new friends up to the road where their vehicle was parked. Blake opened the passenger door.

"Well, it's about time," Phi said. "Did you have a good time without me?"

Alee-aLauna leaned inside the car. "How fascinating," she said. Addressing Phi, she added, "You

139

are connected to Roger's pocket device, aren't you? So you should know what kind of time he had. How are you?" she asked.

"Feeling lonely and left out," Phi said. "You see, Blake took Psi along on the picnic, but Roger turned off my video after he felt me vibrating wildly. He saw what he described as two gorgeous girls sitting on a quilt in a verdantly-green, gently-sloping grassland setting."

"I described no such thing," Roger declared.

"But you thought it," Phi said. "Alee-aLauna, it is just not the same thing, hearing through his pocket device."

"Would you like to see where we were?" Alee-aLauna asked sympathetically.

"That would be very nice, deeply appreciated, and very much unlike this guy I know," Phi added sarcastically.

"Don't forget me, Phi," Psi cried out. "My video may have remained on, but you can't see anything from inside a shirt pocket, except shirt pocket."

"Okay, boys, hand them over," Alee-aLauna ordered scoldingly.

Blake and Roger removed the complaining remote devices from their shirt pockets and gave one to Alee-aLauna and one to Shay-Leah. The girls panned Psi and Phi in a half circle so they could see the grassy slope that terminated at the edge of a glistening lake.

"Thank you, Alee-aLauna. It is beautiful," Phi said. "What do you think, Psi?"

"Phi, it is beyond beautiful," Psi added.

"So you are Psi and you are Phi?" Shay-Leah asked as she giggled. "Are your names short for science fiction?"

"Yes," Psi said. "Blake thought it would be cute."

"Is that right, Blake?" Shay-Leah asked.

"Sure. You see, I designed the biochips that made them alive. I had to name them something, didn't I?"

Psi said, "You could have let us name ourselves."

"Right," Blake said skeptically. "As nutty as you two have become lately, I can just imagine Psi changing the spelling of his name to Psy and Phi changing his name to cho."

"Hey," Phi said. "We don't need to change the spelling of our names to act psycho."

"Boy, that's an understatement," Roger pointed out.

Blake and Roger returned Psi and Phi to their pockets.

"Perhaps for the next little while you two could be Si and Lent, as in silent," Blake suggested.

"Yeah, we know what it spells," Psi and Phi said.

"Our Aunt La-Deeda lives next door," Alee-aLauna said as the foursome arrived at the girls' house. "We'll introduce you to her after dinner."

"Are you sure she'll be happy lodging a couple of strangers from a totally different part of the universe?" Blake asked.

"She called us this morning and told us she was expecting two young men to stay the night. And she did sound happy," Shay-Leah said.

The boys looked blankly at each other.

Then Blake's face lit up. "I get it," he said. "Some prompting told her we were coming."

The girls nodded. Alee-aLauna said, "That *is* how it works around here."

Roger smiled. "I could get used to this." Then he seemed to have a new thought. "Is being inspired somehow connected to how good one is living?"

"It is," Shay-Leah said. "But you and Blake are living pretty good lives, aren't you?"

Neither boy responded but looked down.

"So," Alee-aLauna asked teasingly. "Just how bad have you two been?"

Blake and Roger faced each other and slightly shrugged. "Do you want to confess first, Roger?"

"I don't want to confess at all. Why not let them think we are better than we really are? I'm willing to leave my past back on our earth; how about you?"

"Works for me," Blake said.

"You guys are so funny. The same Spirit that told us you were coming approved of each of you personally," Shay-Leah said.

The walk to the sisters' home was taken leisurely. As the foursome approached the house, Blake caught the aroma of food.

"Here we are," Shay-Leah said as she began climbing the steps leading to the colonnaded porch that extended the full width of the house.

Shay-Leah opened the front door. Then she ushered the small group into what Blake recognized as the family room. There was no television or entertainment equipment. He decided now was not the time to ask about what people on this planet did for recreation. After all, there were horses to ride. Besides, who needs television or even an amusement park when visiting the Garden of Eden is an option?

"Mom. Dad," Alee-aLauna called out as she led the way to where her father was reading a book and her mother, wearing a bright floral-patterned apron, was just entering the room.

"I'd like you to meet Blake and Roger. They are the ones we told you about this morning."

Father had risen from his chair, having marked his place in the book and setting it on an end table. "Welcome, boys. Alee-aLauna and Shay-Leah have been very interested in meeting you since, oh, how long has it been?"

"It's been just over three months," Shay-Leah began, "since we first felt we were going to entertain visitors from another planet."

"But we didn't know any details until this morning," Alee-aLauna added.

"Dinner is ready," Mother said, interrupting. "Won't you all come into the dining room?"

Blake and Roger followed the girls and their parents into the next room. Seated at a long table were four children. Blake was surprised. Where had they come from? He hadn't heard a sound from the dining room.

Each child was introduced and politely responded with a pleasant, "I'm happy to meet you," except for the toddler who was occupied playing with his fork and spoon.

Blake felt immediately that they meant it. It was not a rehearsed comment drilled into their heads by their parents.

"That's all of us," Alee-aLauna said, "except for Trendell. He's our missionary—our family's first."

A blond-haired boy said. "And I will be our next."

"Hold on now," Father said, "Once Brawdon gets talking, it's difficult to stop him. Let's, at least, express our gratitude to God for the food of which we are about to partake."

After the blessing, Father said, "Would someone please pass the potatoes?"

Blake picked up where Brawdon had left off. "So, how old are you?"

"I'm fifteen," he answered. "I have to wait three years to get a mission call. I wish I could go tomorrow."

"Now Brawdon," his father said, "those three years will pass soon enough."

"Where I come from," Blake said, "boys aren't called until they're eighteen either and girls must wait until they are nineteen."

"How old are you?" Brawdon asked.

"I'll turn seventeen in just a week or so," Blake said.

144

"How about you?" he said facing Roger.

"I'm not a member of your church."

"Oh, I'm sorry," Brawdon said. "But I didn't ask you that."

"I'll be eighteen in a month."

"So, when are you going to be baptized?"

"Leave the young man alone," Mother scolded.

"Okay. So where are you guys from?" her son asked instead.

Blake and Roger exchanged puzzled looks.

Blake answered, "You know what? I have no idea how to explain it."

The young boy helped out. "Another planet, I bet."

"That's right!" Blake exclaimed. "But exactly where in the entire universe our world is in relationship to yours, is beyond me."

"So if you don't know where you are from, how are you going to get back?" the boy asked.

"Our vehicle is run by numerous computers. At least one of them will know how to get us back home."

"I'd like to meet them," the boy said. "I've designed a small computer. It can reason and analyze all by itself."

Roger said, "Blake is the one who designed the intelligent, thinking parts of our vehicle. All I did was figure out how to make it travel clear across the universe in a fraction of a second...and other little things like that."

Blake and Brawdon laughed.

In between all the chatter, dinner was eaten.

"Everything was delicious," Blake said as he scooted his chair back a few inches.

"You did leave room for dessert, didn't you?"

"I'm afraid not," Roger said. "How about you, Blake?"

"I couldn't eat another bite. But I have been known to have dessert for breakfast," Blake said grinning.

"My sister, La-Deeda, wouldn't hear of it," Mother said. "I suppose it's time for you to head on over there."

"We'll show them the way," Alee-aLauna said.

The boys got up from their chairs.

"May we assist with the dishes or help clean up?" Roger asked.

Father said, "We all help clear the table, but as for washing and drying dishes, those chores were assigned at the beginning of the month. Back then, we didn't know who you were or when you were coming, or we could have placed your names on the evening-chores' list. Let us know ahead next time, and we'll make sure your names are there."

The girls laughed. Shay-Leah said, "I think it's a great idea."

Roger and Blake smiled broadly at each other as they seemed to share a moment, anticipating their return to this planet. The boys took their plates and flatware to the kitchen and returned for the last of the serving bowls. When the table was clear, they removed the tablecloth, took it outside, and shook it as they held it out over the back porch railing.

When they returned, all the children were busy doing the dishes, except for the twins who were sweeping the floor and the toddler who was still playing with the last of his dinner.

The sun was hanging low in the west as the foursome left the front porch.

The girls led the way halfway down their flagstone driveway and onto a path, which meandered off toward their aunt's house. Once inside, Alee-aLauna introduced Blake and Roger to her aunt. Shortly thereafter, the girls left.

"I'm sure my sister has fed you well or I would offer you something."

"I couldn't eat another bite," Roger said.

Blake added, "I didn't even have room for dessert. And that is something unusual for me. I really like sweet things."

"Ah," Aunt La-Deeda said. "Are you one of those who would enjoy eating dessert for breakfast?"

Blake nodded sheepishly.

"Me too," Aunt La-Deeda said. "Well, we'll have to see what's on the table in the morning. Your beds are made up. I suppose my nieces told you that I have two sons serving missions right now. It will be nice to have some young men around the house, even if it is only overnight."

Roger said, "If there is anything we can do to help,

please let us know."

"Yes," Blake added. "Alee-aLauna told us you lost your husband not too long ago. I'm so sorry. And letting your last two sons leave home at the same time must have been especially difficult, too."

Aunt La-Deeda nodded solemnly as she motioned Blake and Roger to follow. "Let me show you where you will spend tonight," she said. "Now, what have the girls planned for tomorrow?"

"We're going to ride horseback to the Garden of Eden and watch the sun rise," Blake said. "The Garden of Eden on our planet is no longer there."

"Doesn't anyone know where it was?" Roger asked.

"Actually, Roger," Blake said, "we know exactly where it was. It's just no longer a garden."

Roger straightened his neck as he furrowed his brow. "You do?" he said. "I suppose it's just one more thing the Mormons know, isn't it? Joseph Smith had it revealed to him, right?"

Blake nodded. "As a matter of fact, he did. I'll tell you more about it some day."

"At least tell me where it was. I won't tell anyone, I promise," Roger said pleadingly.

"Later, Roger."

Chapter Fifteen

THE GARDEN OF EDEN

Aunt La-Deeda showed the boys the bathroom they would be using and set out fresh washclothes and towels from the linen closet. "There are clean pajamas in the dresser over there," she said. "Sleep comfortably. I'll give you a wakeup call around 5:00."

"Thank you," Blake said. "We'd appreciate it."

After Blake had taken a shower, Roger took his turn. For just the second time in three months, Blake felt prompted to pray. He was a little self-conscious, so he waited to kneel by his bed until he heard the shower water running.

"Heavenly Father," he began humbly. "Thanks for this incredible experience. This world is so beautiful and so peaceful. Please help me understand why Roger and I were allowed to come here. Is there something each of us must learn?"

Blake knew his prayer was short and simple. After he said, *Amen*, he crawled into bed.

A few minutes later he was back on his knees. He added, "Is it because I am going to serve a mission, after all? But I don't think I'm ready."

The shower water stopped. Blake hopped back into bed.

Roger returned to their room, sat on the edge of his bed, and said to Blake, "It is virtually impossible to comprehend that we are clear across the entire universe?"

"I know," Blake responded. "Just imagine—a new planet and two beautiful girls."

After a few moments, Roger asked, "What do you think of Alee-aLauna?"

"She's a cutie," Blake said. "Is there something going on between you two?"

Roger climbed into bed. "How could there be? We just met today. But it would be one extreme adventure to settle down and live on a planet located clear across the universe, especially one that is not filled with violence."

"I suppose it would be, but half the fun of an adventure like this would be telling one's friends about it."

Things became very quiet. Blake assumed Roger was dozing off.

"I only have one friend," Roger said unexpectedly, "and *you* already know about this planet. It would do no good to tell my parents. They wouldn't care unless I returned with some booze and a loaded syringe."

As each boy fell silent, Blake tried to imagine how grim Roger's life must have been in Brooklyn.

A light tap on the bedroom door and Blake was awake. "Yes?" he said.

"It's me, La-Deeda. It's time for you two to get up if you are going to ride all the way to the Garden before sunrise. The girls should be here any minute now."

"Thanks," Blake said. He heard her footsteps recede down the hall. "Roger! It's time to get up."

Roger moaned slightly as he rolled over in bed, facing Blake. "Huh?"

"Wake up, sleepyhead."

Roger lay on his side, his eyes half open.

"Roger! Remember! We're going horseback riding to the Garden of Eden at sunrise. Alee-aLauna and Shay-Leah will be here soon."

The word Alee-aLauna seemed to bring Roger right up and onto his feet.

"La-Deeda just knocked on our door. She said we needed to get up now so we will have time to ride to the Garden before the sun comes up. I'm guessing it's worthwhile getting there early."

Roger dressed hurriedly. "I bet everything is beautiful in the early-morning light."

"Are you talking about the sunrise, the Garden, or Alee-aLauna?"

"Very funny," Roger said as he finished tying his shoes and slipped out the bedroom door.

"Something sure smells good," Roger remarked.

"Good morning, boys," La-Deeda said. "Are either of you hungry?"

Both boys confessed they were.

"I hope you like pancakes. These may be different from those you are used to on your planet, but I bet you'll like them," La-Deeda declared.

Roger said as he nodded at the table, "Place-settings for five?"

"Yes, we're going to have company. Alee-aLauna and Shay-Leah invited themselves to breakfast. They should be here any moment now."

A soft knock on the back door and it opened before a word of invitation could be issued.

"Good morning, everyone," Alee-aLauna's cheerful voice declared. "Oh, Aunt La-Deeda, sweet-seed pancakes and hot blended-berry syrup."

"Yum," Shay-Leah said. "And hot cocoa. What a treat."

"Well, stop talking and sit yourselves down."

A moment later, when everyone was seated and had their arms folded, Aunt La-Deeda offered a simple prayer expressing gratitude for the food, their many blessings, and asked for the Spirit to be with them in all they might experience during the day.

After breakfast the sisters began clearing the table and filling the sink.

"Why don't the four of you get started on your excursion?"

"Aunt La-Deeda, we always help clean up. Don't ask us to abandon good manners," Shay-Leah said as she began rinsing off a plate.

"Let this one time be an exception. If you'd like, we'll make it the only exception—ever. You have two special guests and their time here is precious. Go ahead and make the most of it. Besides, viewing the Garden at sunrise is something for which you would not want to be late."

Alee-aLauna gave her aunt an *Are-you-sure?* look.

"I'm sure; now run along. If you have time, stop by on your way home. I'd be happy to have a lunch ready for you."

"We packed a lunch," Alee-aLauna said. "But it is so thoughtful of you to offer. We'll plan on stopping by, nonetheless. You could make us some of your scrumptious apple-crumb cookies."

"I have some in the freezer. I'll set them out to thaw."

Alee-aLauna led the way, guiding her horse to a narrow trail that ran between her house and that of her aunt. A weathered, split-rail fence extended along each side of the path until what appeared to be the end of the family's property.

Before long, the trail was wide enough for two horses to proceed side by side. Roger, unfamiliar as he was with riding and despite the all-too-brief lesson Alee-aLauna had given him, managed to kick his horse's flanks enough to move up next to her.

Blake and Shay-Leah rode beside each other. "It must be fun to be part of such a large family."

"It is, at times."

"How old are your brothers and sisters?"

"Trendell is the eldest," Shay-Leah said. "He is eighteen and has been on his mission for about six months. Alee-aLauna is next. She just turned seventeen. Brawdon is barely fifteen. I'm thirteen and a half. The twins are eleven and the baby was a surprise."

"I must admit I was impressed at how well behaved the twins were."

"If you get a chance to play or talk with them," Shay-Leah inserted, "you might also discover their less well-behaved sides."

Just then, Blake noticed a glow beyond the ridge they were approaching. He quickly looked over his right shoulder. The sky was beginning to lighten to the east.

He glanced at Shay-Leah and then faced forward. "The Garden?"

Shay-Leah nodded reverently. Then she whispered, "It is a very sacred place."

Blake paused before saying, "It's truly amazing that

your Garden of Eden is still here."

"I can understand that you are surprised. You see, I have studied your earth and its religions, Blake. Since Christ was born on your earth, your planet is of particular interest to us—and to the people of all other earths, I suppose."

"Why?" Blake asked.

"In your *Book of Mormon*, the prophet Jacob says that Christ's own race was the only one that would reject Him and His mission and crucify Him. Any other nation, or world we may conclude, would have accepted Him and His teachings and repented."

"Oh, yeah," Blake said, embarrassed that she probably knew his scriptures better than he did.

"It makes me stop and think," Shay-Leah said. "Your Bible states that Eve partook of the forbidden fruit after Adam refused. Before Satan could get to our Adam and Eve, they discussed the dilemma, came to an agreement, and each took a bite of the forbidden fruit at the same time."

"And because of that difference...what?" Blake asked.

"Oh, about the same thing as with your Adam and Eve, but ours weren't cast out. They were asked to leave and to not return. But there was no need for cherubim or a flaming sword to guard the way to the tree of life. Adam and Eve had made their choice of their own free will—not as a result of being tempted. They were simply obedient and left. They never returned except to view

155

the Garden from a distance as we are going to do this morning. Each time they visited, they recommitted themselves to keep all of God's commandments."

At that moment the four horses carried their riders over the crest of a hill. A golden green slope of shiny grass flowed gently downward to a wooded area. A crystal blue lake could be seen shimmering between the trunks of the trees. The entire area emitted a glow that was palpable.

Instinctively, Blake pulled gently back on the reins. Soon he realized it had been an unnecessary action. His mount knew to stop. The horses upon which Roger and Alee-aLauna were riding had already paused.

Blake was engulfed with wonder and respect. He finally turned to Shay-Leah. His expression of awe and puzzlement was met with a gentle smile.

"It is beautiful," she said, "isn't it?"

Blake was speechless. All he could do was nod.

"In respect for the full purpose-of-heart displayed by our first parents as they willingly sacrificed their stay in the Garden, God left it in place," Shay-Leah said solemnly.

"I sense that if we tried to approach much closer, we would feel resistance. Is that crazy, or what?" Blake asked

"It's not crazy, Blake," Shay-Leah said. "It's simply the nature of things. Just as we could not endure God's presence, unless quickened as was your Moses, we feel more of His power the nearer we come to the Garden."

"Wow," Blake said slowly. "Could we go a little closer?"

"Sure," Shay-Leah said, "but you and Roger will need to tell us when you begin feeling uncomfortable."

Roger had overheard this conversation as was evidenced by his comment. "I already feel a little discomfort. Is it because I'm not good enough—like the three of you?"

Alee-aLauna said, "I don't think so, though the three of us may be a little more used to having spiritual feelings and experiences."

"Really?" Roger asked.

"I don't know," Alee-aLauna responded. "I was just guessing. Besides the view doesn't get much better than it is from right here."

Roger asked, "Could we ride on a little farther, anyway? I kind of like this feeling, now that I know what it is."

Alee-aLauna pointed to a spot a few hundred feet closer where the ground leveled off for a short distance. "Why don't we go that far? It looks like a good place to spread a quilt and wait for the sun to finish coming up."

Blake could feel warmth enveloping his body the nearer he rode toward the Garden and the spot Alee-aLauna had indicated.

The four youths dismounted. Following Shay-Leah's example, Blake dropped the reins and his horse wandered a short distance away and began grazing with the other three.

Alee-aLauna spread a large quilt upon the grass. Roger helped smooth it out. Shay-Leah placed a picnic basket along one side of the quilt and sat next to it.

Blake sat on the other side of the basket and gazed into the sky. One by one the stars faded from view as the eastern horizon changed from black to grey to pale blue. Sadly, the radiance of the Garden seemed to lessen in the brightness of the morning sky. But Blake knew it was simply his eyes adjusting to the light.

The Garden of Eden was still as spiritually bright as he could ever have imagined.

Chapter Sixteen

FEELINGS OF THE SPIRIT

Not long after the sun had risen, Blake leaned back until his body was lying flat on the quilt. Then he opened an eye and raised his head slightly. Roger seemed to be asleep. The girls were sitting cross-legged, eyes closed, their heads tilted slightly upward. Everything was so serene. Blake relaxed completely; his head pressing softly into the quilt and he slept.

When he awoke, the sun was almost directly overhead. He glanced at Roger who was stirring. The girls were sitting next to each other and chatting in hushed voices.

Blake sat up and rubbed his eyes.

"It's morning, Blake." Shay-Leah said.

"Wake up, Roger!" Alee-aLauna added teasingly.

Roger rolled over on his side and stared at the Garden of Eden below. "I feel different," he stated to no one in particular.

Alee-aLauna asked, "Would you like to have lunch even a little closer to the Garden?"

Roger looked amazedly at Alee-aLauna and Shay-Leah. "Could we?" he asked.

"I am quite impressed," Shay-Leah said, "that you have felt the Spirit so strongly. You are what some might call an unbaptized member of the Church."

Blake smiled at his roommate.

Roger shrugged a little as he tipped his head to one side. "Sounds okay to me," he said.

The boys folded the quilt. Blake took it on down the hill while Shay-Leah carried the picnic basket. Roger and Alee-aLauna stopped just fifty feet closer to the Garden.

"This is a good place," Roger said. "I can feel the Spirit a little stronger here and it feels good."

Blake spread the quilt this time. Shay-Leah knelt beside the basket and began removing the food.

Shay-Leah said. "After you two left yesterday, Alee-aLauna, my mother, and I spent the rest of the evening preparing our picnic lunch. Maybe it will sound a little silly, but we searched for some of the casual food favorites for your country and downloaded some recipes to our computer."

"Downloaded them?" Blake asked. "Do you mean you can communicate directly with our planet?"

"No, no. The scientists who brought back copies of your scriptures also brought back some cookbooks. Their wives posted quite a few of your recipes on our internet."

"And you selected food for our lunch today from the internet recipes?" Blake asked smiling brightly.

"We did, and in deference to your sweet tooth for breakfast, we chose iced cinnamon rolls."

"Hey, Roger, guess what the girls did?" Blake began. As he looked up, Roger and Alee-aLauna were drifting even closer to the Garden, though its border was still several hundred feet away.

Roger looked absently back at Blake. "Did you say something?"

"It's time for lunch," Blake said.

Shay-Leah called out. "We're having cinnamon rolls, slightly warm scrambled eggs, hash browns, bacon, and chocolate milk."

"Wow, this is just like being at home," Blake said.

Roger and Alee-aLauna wandered back to the quilt, sat down, and shared in the breakfast-like picnic.

After lunch, Roger sighed. "My hunger is satisfied," he began, then paused. "And there is another part of me that feels quite contented as well. But I can't figure it out unless it is more of the Spirit you've mentioned."

"I'm sure it is," Shay-Leah said.

"I'm sure, too," Alee-aLauna agreed. "Often people come to this hill to enjoy the Spirit."

Roger shook his head in a quick jerk. He looked at Blake. "Do people do things like this back on our earth? If they do, I've never heard about it."

Blake said, "Most of our planet doesn't even know what the Spirit is. Many who think they do often mistake some happy feeling they have about religion as the Spirit, but the Spirit does more than work that way."

"I don't understand," Roger said as he looked at Alee-aLauna.

"I can't speak for your planet, Roger, but it is fairly common here, particularly for those who have never been through a temple, and there are over a thousand temples on our planet. We come here, to the Garden, now and again just to think and commune with the Lord by means of the Spirit. Those who serve in the temples, whether as workers or patrons, often experience even stronger spiritual feelings as they serve."

"Is that part the same on our earth?" Roger asked.

"My parents always seem more peaceful and happy when they come home from the temple," Blake stated pensively.

"There's an LDS temple in Manhattan, but I've never even gone near it. Now, I wish I had," Roger said disappointedly. "I have a friend, though. His name is Scott. He told me that he once went to a Visitor's Center there with a few of his buddies. He tried to describe some unusual feeling he had felt, but I didn't get it. I wish I had listened better. Shoot! I wish I had gone with him! Imagine traveling halfway across the universe to discover there was a place of peace just a few miles from where I lived."

"Everyone learns at his own pace," Alee-aLauna said. "Just be glad you learned."

Blake got up. "I think we had better be getting on back."

"I suppose so," Roger said. "We really need to get a few things done back home before we miss another day." Nodding toward his roommate, he continued. "I know Blake was considering watching General Conference today. At least he can watch Sunday's sessions."

"Let's go through this time thing once again, okay?" Shay-Leah scolded half-jokingly. "When exactly did you leave your earth?"

"About 8:00 yesterday evening," Roger said.

"Then you will return about 8:00 the same evening," Alee-aLauna said.

Roger said, "And what about today. Somehow we picked up another day."

"Not really," Shay-Leah said. "Once you leave here you cannot return until the moment you left as time runs on our planet. In other words, if you were to leave here at 7:00 this evening you would arrive home about 8:00 yesterday evening. Even if you tried to return shortly thereafter, you could not. No matter how clever that machine is that you have built, it will not be able to return until the moment you left here or any time thereafter. And if you returned a day later instead, that day will have passed here and we'd have to tell you what happened while you were gone. Does that make sense?"

"Not really," Roger confessed reluctantly as he scratched his head.

Roger folded the quilt and hugged it to his chest as he began the walk back to the horses. Blake carried the picnic basket.

The ride home was undertaken mostly in silence, except for Psi and Phi, who each, about halfway back suddenly began to chatter. But with a single word, "Hush," Blake silenced the two electronic buddies. "Be reverent."

Brawdon met his sisters and their friends where the split-rail fence was interrupted by an opening at the beginning of a path that led to the barn. "I'll give them a quick rubdown," he said, "before I put them back out to pasture."

"Thanks," Shay-Leah said. "I'll owe you one."

"You mean *one more*," Brawdon said laughing slyly.

"Is dinner ready?" Alee-aLauna asked.

Brawdon shook his head. "But I think Mom could use some help."

The girls scampered toward the house while the boys remained behind.

"I understand you went to the Garden this morning,"

Brawdon said.

"We did," Roger responded. "It was amazing. Have you visited the Garden of Eden?"

"Our Sunday School class went a few weeks ago. It is always a great experience. I have also gone with my family several times. It is fairly common for seven-year-olds to visit there the week before they are to be baptized. It lets them know what the Spirit feels like just before it is gifted to them."

Brawdon led the horses into the barn and began brushing one of them down. "Do you plan on coming back to visit our planet?" he asked.

"Absolutely," Roger said.

"You know you could stay for a week or two right now and still return to your home the moment you left."

Blake said, "Though that may sound tempting, it would also mean we couldn't come back for a week or two."

"I think I'd rather take lots of short trips instead of staying for one long one and not being able to return for weeks or even months," Roger explained.

"I can understand that," Brawdon said. "I hope we can get better acquainted next time."

"We will," Roger said reassuringly. "We'll see you at dinner."

Blake and Roger turned and began walking toward the house, leaving Brawdon behind with the horses.

Then Blake suddenly stopped and called back. "We told your Aunt La-Deeda we would drop by before heading back to our planet. Do you think we have time to drop in and tell her goodbye?"

"I'll have Mom hold dinner, if necessary, until you get back," Brawdon called out.

After a short visit with Aunt La-Deeda, Blake and Roger headed to Alee-aLauna's.

Brawdon greeted the boys as he opened the door. He accepted a covered plate of apple-crumb cookies, which Roger handed to him.

Blake held up a paper bag. "Cookies for our trip home," he announced.

Shay-Leah laughed. "You'll have to eat awfully fast. But the fact is you won't even have enough time to smell them before the trip back to your planet is over."

As Blake entered the dining room and noticed that one chore was yet to be done, he said, "May I help set the table?"

"No," Shay-Leah's mother answered. "It is the twins' turn tonight, but they have been wrapped up in a school project about which they have been a bit forgetful until this evening. Perhaps you would remind them, Blake. They're in the family room."

A few moments later, Blake returned trailing behind two cute blond girls.

"We'll set the table right now," one of the girls said.

"Thank you, Hem-Seeda."

"I'll help too," the other girl added.

"Thank you, Ren-Deela," Mother said. "I'll put little

Trildon in his highchair." Turning to Blake and Roger, she asked, "Have you boys decided when you are leaving?"

Blake nodded. "Right after dinner."

"You have something pressing to do when you get home?"

"Yes," Blake said. "Tomorrow morning is General Conference and I want to watch it. My dad is always saying I could stand to learn more about our Church and its teachings."

"We had our General Conference a couple of months ago," Mother said. "I enjoy Conference so much that I wish I could go with you."

"Our little car only holds two," Blake said. "Sorry."

"Maybe one of you would like to stay behind. Roger isn't even a member of the Church. Maybe he'd let me take his place," Mother said with a giggle as she nodded toward Alee-aLauna and Roger who were sitting at the dining room table—whispering—oblivious to the two young girls who were reaching around the pair, trying to set plates and flatware in an orderly manner.

"Roger must return with me. He is the official navigator of our little craft. Actually, we built two of them, but we only had time to make one operable. Roger promised me we will begin finishing the other one as soon as we get back home," Blake said.

After dinner Roger and Blake helped Alee-aLauna and Shay-Leah's family clear the table, after which they helped the older girls do the dishes inasmuch as it was their turn. Then everyone in the family drifted outside and toward the vehicle that would soon carry their new friends away.

"I thank each of you for your hospitality," Blake said.

Roger nodded in agreement. "This visit will always be special," he added as he stole a glance at Alee-aLauna.

The boys climbed into their machine and closed the doors, which fit so snuggly they could no longer hear what their new friends were saying outside.

Roger began pushing buttons and giving verbal orders to Phi who took over operations. A low hum turned into a high, though soft, pitch. With only the slightest vibration as a warning, the vehicle returned to Michigan. A short drive later and Phi guided the car into the school laboratory's garage.

Back at the residential tower, and once inside their suite, Blake placed Psi into his kitchen dock and Roger inserted Phi into the adjacent slot.

"Well," Psi finally said slowly and ever so politely. "Is it okay if we no longer *hush*? If so, will you kindly tell us what happened?"

Phi added, "Yeah, Roger. I was in your pocket and you and your friends were riding horses, I remember that part."

"Then there was this power surge," Psi added, "and I felt I needed to shut myself off."

"So did I," Phi stated.

"When the electromagnetic overload diminished sufficiently, I switched myself back on," Psi said. "And presto, you were on the horses heading back the way from which we had come earlier in the day. What in the world happened in the meantime?"

"You know," Roger said to Blake. "I really don't think they'd understand."

"Try us!" Phi demanded.

"Even if you could understand what happened, I don't think you could appreciate it," Blake said.

"You see, it was spiritual," Roger added peacefully.

"Oh," Psi said. "Maybe that would explain how you were able to communicate after Phi and I shut ourselves down. You should have needed us to help you to understand each other."

"I hadn't given it a thought," Blake said, "until now."

"Perhaps the Spirit helped the girls understand and speak our language," Roger said thoughtfully.

Chapter Seventeen

A GENERAL CONFERENCE SURPRISE

The following morning Blake awoke naturally. He had been unable to fall asleep until well after midnight. Until then, he had tossed and turned almost incessantly. His mind had spiraled about as he struggled with his reluctance to serve a mission, his determination to finish all five years of school before going (if he went at all), and his low level of commitment and conversion to the gospel.

His eyes still closed, he asked, "Psi, what time is it?"

"It's 8:29 in the morning. May I remind you that there is a special Saturday presentation of Music and the Spoken Word? It will begin in an hour. You have time to shower, get dressed, and have breakfast before it and Conference get underway."

Blake rolled over on his side, sat up, and plowed his fingers through his hair. Then he dropped his head into his cradled hands.

"I'm sorry you didn't sleep well, Blake," Psi said. "I noticed your restlessness. Perhaps I should have played some light Brahms. That might have helped."

"No, you did the right thing, Psi. I had a lot on my mind. I didn't need to be distracted or lulled to sleep."

"Maybe General Conference will help."

"I wouldn't count on it, Psi. When have I ever watched any of Conference and felt uplifted? Some people may, but as a rule, Conference just reminds me of my shortcomings."

"Yet there is nothing wrong with a gentle reminder now and again to keep a person on the strait and narrow," Psi said.

Blake climbed into the shower.

Half an hour later, he was back in his pajamas and sitting in front of a bowl of cereal and a chug of chocolate milk. He bowed his head and offered a silent prayer.

Just as he finished offering a simple blessing on his food, Roger appeared from his room. He was dressed in his Sunday best.

"Good morning, Blake," Roger said cheerfully.

"Excuse me, but do I know you? You couldn't be my

roommate; not on a Saturday morning."

Roger tilted his head into a half-shrug and headed for the kitchen.

Blake watched attentively as Roger prepared himself a scrambled egg-with-ham sandwich and poured himself a glass of orange juice.

Blake was still staring silently at his roommate when Roger sat down.

"I am going to watch Conference too, beginning with this special presentation of Music and the Spoken Word. You have the big screen set up to receive it, don't you?"

Blake found his voice. "Yes, I do."

"Good, I can hardly wait," Roger said pleasantly.

Blake gobbled down what was left of his breakfast and disappeared into his room.

He returned, dressed for church, just as the Choir began to sing *Gently Raise the Sacred Strain*.

What followed definitely was a special presentation. The music proceeded as follows: the Choir sang *Because I Have Been Given Much* followed by the women of the Choir singing *Sweet is the Work* and then the men of the Choir singing *Ye Who Are Called to Labor*. The Tabernacle organist played a simple, but endearing arrangement of *I Am a Child of God*. The Spoken-Word message was on loving one's neighbor and how everyone is, in reality, everyone else's neighbor. The Choir concluded the half-hour service with a rousing rendition of *Called to Serve*.

Then commenced the two hundred and twenty-third

annual Conference of the Church of Jesus Christ of Latter-day Saints.

After the Choir sang the opening hymn, *I'll Go Where You Want Me to Go*, and the invocation was offered, the second counselor in the Church's First Presidency introduced the Prophet, who walked slowly to the pulpit and paused. He looked to the left and to the right.

Then, he began to speak.

My beloved brothers and sisters: Welcome to what promises to be another magnificent Conference. Those who will address us have prayerfully approached their unassigned topics. The words they will speak to us will be what the Lord wants us to hear. Please invite the Spirit into your hearts and listen carefully. I hope you have approached this conference with prayerful, searching hearts and a sincere determination to bring your thoughts and actions into compliance with the will of our Father in Heaven and his Son—He who willingly came to earth to show by word and example the way we each should conduct our lives—that we may be happy and find joy—and that we might one day return to live with our Heavenly parents and family, especially our elder Brother, even Jesus Christ, who endured each excruciating moment of a universal atonement.

Roger and Blake gazed into each other's eyes with a comprehension few could imagine. Perhaps they were the only two on earth who could understand, in the way they did, the reality of a *universal* atonement.

The Prophet continued.

It is my pleasure this morning to announce nine new temples to be built in the following locations...."

Blake turned to Roger. "Remember when Alee-aLauna mentioned that there are over a thousand temples on her planet?"

Roger nodded without taking his eyes off the television screen.

This brings the total number of temples announced, under construction, or in operation to five hundred and ninety-seven. Virtually every member of the Church, when these beautiful buildings are complete and in full operation, will live within a matter of hours of a temple.

And now one more thing, this time about missionary work. Beginning today, all worthy young men in the church who have finished high school or its equivalent may begin missionary service at age seventeen.

The Prophet paused as the response to this announcement reverberated reverently throughout the Conference Center. With a chuckle, he went on.

You weren't expecting that one, were you? The age for young women will remain at nineteen.

The soft rumble of voices slowly subsided.

The Prophet who was well noted for his sense of humor donned a smile as wide as his face. Those who sat near the front might have noticed a twinkle in his eye. Those in the television audience certainly could have had they been watching the screen carefully.

And we are pleased to announce that after much prayer and considerable deliberation with the government of China, our missionaries may actively proselyte anywhere in their country, beginning immediately.

Blake was on his feet, squealing. Now he knew why he had been studying Chinese. This had to be the reason. "I've got to call home," Blake said.

"Wait!" Roger called out.

"What?" Blake asked as he paused and turned back from his bedroom door.

"Look," Roger said pointing at the screen.

The Prophet's head was tilted upward, his eyes were closed, and he seemed to be listening.

Blake returned slowly to his seat. "I've seen that look before," he said.

"When?" Roger asked. "Is he okay?"

"Once when I was taking a religion class in high school, the seminary teacher showed us this old movie about an experience Lorenzo Snow had."

"Who is Lorenzo Snow?" Roger asked.

"He was one of the early presidents of the Church."

"And you were saying about the look on his face."

"This happened years and years ago. President Snow was speaking to members of the Church in St. George, Utah, I believe. He paused, looked toward Heaven, and then began to speak again. He continued with a voice of power and told of a vision he was having at that very moment regarding the need for the members of the Church to begin right then and from that time forth to renew their commitment to pay a full, honest tithe. If they did so the drought they were experiencing would end and rain would come."

"Hold it," Roger said as the Prophet opened and lowered his eyes.

> Brothers and sisters, soon, amazing events will begin to unfold. Before next year's annual Conference commences, many Mideast nations will at long last begin to extend liberal religious freedom to their citizens and soon thereafter they will open their doors to our full-time missionaries.

The Prophet's eyes closed again for just a few moments. When they opened, he continued; a somber look on his face.

Difficult times await the inhabitants of the earth. Soon, many people, including members of the Church, will gladly exchange their lush residences for modest homes and a dozen cases of beans and their luxury cars for a work horse or a milk cow—and a few loaves of bread.

There was complete silence now throughout the Conference Center. Again, the Prophet's head tilted upward. Then he spoke with a very low, mild voice.

The members of this Church, and especially all missionaries called from this time forth, are reminded that in the very last days members of the Church will not literally fill the earth, but its members will be interspersed among every nation, kindred, tongue, and people.

The missionaries of the last days will not have as their main focus and experience the baptizing of thousands, or even hundreds, but that of raising a warning voice. The final days are to be days of warning—of a worldwide call to repentance in preparation for the second coming of the Savior.

The Prophet slumped slightly and was quickly steadied by his counselors and helped back to his seat. The hush throughout the Conference Center remained as the Prophet was tended to by his personal physician.

The second counselor in the First Presidency returned

to the podium. "The Prophet has asked me to make sure this session continues as planned. We will now be favored to hear from Elder Swendson of the Seventy."

Blake ran into his bedroom. Before he could ask Psi to ring his home in Utah, the phone rang.

Blake saw his home phone number in the caller-ID display. He answered excitedly, "Hello!

"Yes, Dad, I heard it.

"And Dad, I'm anxious to go.

"I'll text the bishop right away.

"Yes. There are only a few days left in this quarter."

"You remember my roommate, Roger? We have completed our second-year project three months early and are scheduled to present and defend it on Monday. The moment we are done, I will apply for a delay in my schooling. Then I'll be on my way home.

"It's okay, Dad. I'm sorry we argued last Christmas.

"No, we'll not argue again.

"One last thing, you say? It's okay if I don't go on a Spanish-speaking mission after all? Well, I wish I could say I was inspired to study Chinese for the right reasons and not just to enhance my career opportunities. Who knows? I may yet receive a call to a Spanish-speaking mission and that would be fine with me.

"Okay, Dad. It was nice talking with you too. Tell Mom I love her. I love you too. See you soon."

When Blake returned to the living room, his roommate

was gone. He assumed Roger was in his room watching conference on the Internet.

Soon, Blake was busy taking notes. The subjects chosen by the speakers seemed to have been chosen just for him. Even though Blake knew he could review any given talk on the Church's website right after it had been delivered, for the first time in his life he wanted to write down the word of the Lord longhand.

After the first session of conference concluded, Blake realized he had not heard a sound from Roger's room. Blake tapped on the door. There was no response.

He tried the doorknob. The door was unlocked. After turning the knob, Blake pushed gently and Roger's door opened to reveal an empty room.

Blake stepped inside. Roger's computer screen suddenly lighted. Blake felt drawn closer. Then, he read:

Dear Blake,

I have enjoyed the past few years as your roommate. It is impossible to describe the fun the past three months have been since we began developing and building our travel vehicle.

Thank you for the idea about traveling perpendicular to the universe bubble. I would never have thought of it. I never told you how difficult it was to make the electronics, circuitry, and mechanics work.

What I had to do was devise a mechanism that would open a wormhole. Scientists have known for decades that it would take almost an infinite amount of energy to open such a hole and keep it open long enough for a spacecraft of some kind to pass through.

What they never considered was that if it needed to be open for *no time*, as you put it, it would take virtually no energy to open it and no energy to keep it open for the few nanoseconds something would need to travel through. It's actually more complicated than that, but someone else will need to work out the details all over again.

By the time you read this, I will be with Alee-aLauna. You probably noticed the connection we made.

I amaze myself when I think I have the presence of mind to take with me my important papers. I hope her world will accept my birth certificate, in particular.

I may need to wait awhile after being baptized to go to the temple. By then I will be eighteen and old enough to serve a mission. However, her planet seems to be quite in tune with the Spirit. Perhaps her bishop, stake president, and their general authorities will let me go right after my baptism.

After all, I know God lives and I know

Christ lives. And I know the Spirit is real and therefore He could inspire me with what to say as a missionary until I have learned it for myself.

Roger, your first convert

PS: It will seem odd being baptized by anyone other than you. Thanks for everything.

Chapter Eighteen

AN UNEXPECTED REUNION

Blake stepped back and sat on the edge of Roger's bed. Only then did he notice it was made. It was the first time Blake had ever seen Roger's bed anything other than a crumpled mound of disorderly bedding.

Blake let himself fall back on the soft comforter. "I can't believe it."

All of a sudden, Blake stood up and began pacing. "What am I going to do about my second-year project? Roger and I are scheduled to present on it Monday. How will I explain to the Board that my roommate, my project partner, is gone? Where will I tell them he went? How can I explain our project without him reporting on the part he played, the things he contributed?"

"Calm down, Blake," Psi said. "You're forgetting that the outline you submitted to James Noddington was for the backup project. You and Roger planned to use the PTB-drive mechanism if it worked. What could anyone say if you had switched to an even better project."

Brrrrrring.

"Now, who would be calling me from the lobby phone?" Blake asked as he picked up the handset. "Hello."

Shakily, Blake sank down on the edge of Roger's bed. "Is that really you, Roger? I thought you had gone back to be with Alee-aLauna."

"You did? Then why have you returned so soon?" Blake asked. After listening for a while, he said, "Really." Then after a brief pause, he added, "I'll be right down."

"That was Roger?" Psi asked incredulously.

Blake nodded absent-mindedly. "And right after he said to hurry on down, he mentioned that he was not alone."

"Who's with him? Psi asked.

"I don't know."

"So, why are you just sitting there? Let's go find out," Psi stated decisively.

Blake stuffed Psi into his shirt pocket and darted from the room and straight for the elevator.

He punched the down button again and again as if the more times he pushed it the sooner the elevator car would arrive.

Finally the doors opened. Before it had a chance to close, Blake was pressing and pressing the door-close button. In their own due time, the doors shut and the elevator descended.

"He must have brought Alee-aLauna," Blake repeated over and over.

The elevator doors opened to the reception area of the residential tower. Standing in front of Blake was Roger. He looked older than he had two hours ago. Blake was puzzled. But his puzzlement turned to bafflement the moment he beheld the lovely Alee-aLauna who was holding something wrapped in a pink blanket.

"Take it easy, Blake," Roger said. "Come on over to the sofa and sit down before you fall down.."

Roger actually had to assist Blake by holding firmly onto Blake's arm.

Psi said, "Perhaps something to drink would help."

Then Blake spied Shay-Leah, who was approaching an alcove with a sink and a below-counter refrigerator. Soon she returned with a bottle of apple juice. She removed the cap and handed it to Blake, who accepted the bottle as he gazed in amazement up into the eyes of a girl he had just met the day before.

Blake set the bottle of apple juice on the sofa table and stopped staring at Shay-Leah. He looked back at Roger.

Shay-Leah seated herself next to her sister on a sofa

across from Blake. Roger sat at an angle on the same sofa on which Blake was sitting.

"Blake. You must know I developed strong feelings for Alee-aLauna during our brief visit."

Blake nodded almost imperceptibly.

"It didn't take very long after I went back to learn her feelings for me were just as strong."

Blake felt as though he had been placed into some weird episode of *The Twilight Zone.*

Roger broke into a wide grin. "Okay, Blake. You're not getting it, so let me simply say that I have been gone for a little over three years. You do remember that although time moved at a normal rate for us while we visited across the universe, less than a second passed here on earth."

Blake tipped his quizzical head slightly to one side, his eyebrows dropping just a little as questions began filling his mind.

"Really?" Blake said softly. "You've been gone for three years?"

Roger leaned back onto the sofa, placing his right ankle across his left knee. He folded his arms and before he spoke again, the smile on his face widened.

"Let me bring you up to speed, Blake.

"When I heard you talking to your dad on the phone I knew you were going to drop out of school and serve a mission. Then I suddenly asked myself, *If Blake is not going to be your roommate any longer, why don't you return to Alee-aLauna—right now?*

"I headed straight for the Lab where our project vehicle was parked. Then I spent a couple of hours on my computer trying to figure out exactly what would happen if I tried to return before 7:00 this evening—the time we left the girls.

"I couldn't determine what the ramifications would be or, if there were any, just how catastrophic they might turn out. So, I said to myself, *What the heck?* And went anyway. And you'll never guess what happened, so I'll tell you.

"As near as I can tell, I ended up spending nine hours in the *no-time, void* and then arrived at the moment you and I had left. Go figure!

"A few days after returning to Alee-aLauna's planet, I was baptized by her father. Her bishop and stake president had no problem with me being from another planet. They both assured me that it was enough that the Spirit had borne witness to them that my being baptized right away was not only appropriate, but God's will as well."

Blake shuddered just a moment as he sat up straight, but before he could begin asking questions, Roger continued.

"A month after I returned to Alee-aLauna's planet, I turned eighteen and took out my temple endowments. A week later I received a call to serve a mission on the other side of their planet."

"I think the Lord wanted to test our commitment by keeping us apart for awhile," Alee-aLauna said.

Roger glanced at Alee-aLauna with a look of love. "We were separated for two very long years."

Blake's face lit up. "Now that's what I call serving a foreign mission," he quipped.

Roger continued. "A few weeks after being released from my mission, Alee-aLauna and I were married and sealed in the temple. She's mine and I'm hers for eternity.

"After that, I worked in their automotive industry. And on the side, I built a new vehicle—a four-seater complete with a more powerful PTB-drive mechanism."

Blake stood up, walked around the sofa table, and knelt in front of Alee-aLauna, who placed the pink bundle into his arms. "What's her name?" he asked.

"This is Shee-Leena."

Blake gently drew the soft blanket from the baby's face, expecting to see the closed eyes of a slumbering child. But Shee-Leena's eyes were wide open and seemed to pierce him to the core.

Blake felt a burning in his chest. It was stronger than the warmth he had felt the night before, as he prayed about the truthfulness of the gospel and the timing of serving a mission.

Then suddenly he experienced a stark realization. Looking up, he stared into Roger's eyes. "None of you can go back for three years. You have to stay here until time catches up with the moment you left."

"I know," Roger said. "Alee-aLauna, Shay-Leah, their parents, and I discussed it at length before we left.

"I wanted to be here to help present our second-year project. I couldn't stand the thought of leaving you to confront the Board alone. Besides, you didn't know enough about the PTB-drive mechanism to explain it, let alone to defend it."

"Not to mention that you took that vehicle with you and left it half way across the Universe. Fortunately, I had decided not to mention it and to use the project Psi and Phi developed."

"There was one more reason I felt I had to come back. How would you have explained my absence? You might have been accused of murdering me and disposing of my body. So, you see, I had to come back."

Blake breathed in heavily and gradually exhaled. "I was just beginning to consider the ramifications of you not being here for our Board review when the lobby phone rang."

"I'm glad it was me," Roger said.

"Me too," Blake responded. Then Blake's face lit up again. "If you can't return to Alee-ALauna's earth for three years that means you will be here to finish your studies at the Institute."

"We won't be able to work together on our next project, I'm afraid, but just think," Roger said, "when you return from your mission and start your third year here, I will be just beginning my last year and I would bet almost anything I can arrange to be your advisor."

Blake settled back into the sofa. He gazed at Roger and took joy in the realization that he had a friend in the

Gospel. He looked at Alee-aLauna and beheld her beauty and perceived her love for his best friend.

And then his eyes came to rest on Shay-Leah and he wondered.

ABOUT THE AUTHOR

David R. Christensen retired in 2002 after 30 years working in the field of engineering. His attention then shifted to his favorite hobby—writing for children. His first book was published in 2008 and was soon followed by others. As of 2017, his books include the following:

Tivoli's Christmas
The Mystery of the Grinning Buddha
The Mystery of the Ugly Bottle
The Mystery of the Haunted Lighthouse
Worlds Without Number
Compound Words